Those Scandalous Stricklands

From the edge of disgrace to the altar!

The three Strickland sisters,
Faith, Hope and Charity,
have lived with their grandmother, the dowager countess of Comstock, since their parents' deaths. But they are only now realizing just how close they are to being scandalously penniless!

Each sister has her own plan to save the family from disgrace—until they meet the gentlemen who will change their plans, and their lives, forever...

Read Faith's story in

"Her Christmas Temptation"

Part of the *Regency Christmas Wishes* anthology

Read Hope's story in

A Kiss Away from Scandal

Read Charity's story in

How Not to Marry an Earl

All available now!

Author Note

For this book I did more than my usual amount of odd research, including a lot of comparison in the differences in life for my American hero and my English heroine. Adding an American meant that, for the first time ever, I managed to sneak in things that never belong in a Regency, like mentions of a raccoon, whiskey and lots and lots of corn.

But I was also surprised to discover that when my hero and heroine played billiards, there might have been a major difference. There is a theory that the practice of hitting a billiard ball off center to make it spin was something that was introduced to America by the English.

That is why, though it is called "side" in the UK, on my side of the Atlantic we speak of "putting English on the ball."

CHRISTINE MERRILL

How Not to Marry an Earl

Recycling programs for this product may not exist in your area.

ISBN-13: 978-1-335-05185-1

How Not to Marry an Earl

This edition published by arrangement with Harlequin Books S.A.

For questions and comments about the quality of this book, please contact us at CustomerService@Harlequin.com.

Printed in U.S.A.

Christine Merrill lives on a farm in Wisconsin with her husband, two sons and too many pets—all of whom would like her to get off the computer so they can check their email. She has worked by turns in theater costuming and as a librarian. Writing historical romance combines her love of good stories and fancy dress with her ability to stare out the window and make stuff up.

Books by Christine Merrill

Harlequin Historical

Wish Upon a Snowflake
"The Christmas Duchess"
The Secrets of Wiscombe Chase
The Wedding Game

Those Scandalous Stricklands

Regency Christmas Wishes
"Her Christmas Temptation"
A Kiss Away from Scandal
How Not to Marry an Earl

The Society of Wicked Gentlemen

A Convenient Bride for the Soldier

The de Bryun Sisters

The Truth About Lady Felkirk
A Ring from a Marquess

Visit the Author Profile page
at Harlequin.com for more titles.

To Caffeine, without whom this book could not have been written. Don't ever leave me again.

Chapter One

It seemed as if Miles Strickland had been running for ages. First, it had been from Prudence in Philadelphia, to avoid the plans she had made for them. Then the Shawnee, during his brief idea to go West and seek his fortune.

He had run from the Iroquois on the way back.

He had been two steps from the altar and one step away from debtors' prison when the letter had arrived from England and convinced him that his luck had finally turned. His kin had been American far longer than that country had existed and in none of that time had they mentioned the noble family tree they had sprouted from. But now, the British branches had died, leaving him heir to lands and a title.

Visions of wealth and comfort filled his head as he boarded the ship to cross the Atlantic. And then, he'd spoiled it all by actually becoming the Earl of Comstock. Apparently, the English Stricklands were no better off than the Americans. His family's debts had been minuscule compared to the ones attached to his new title. And there was no hope in clearing them, since a lord was not supposed to work. Instead, he was expected to collect rent from tenants even poorer than he was and take a seat in a government he knew nothing about. His brother, Edward, had been lucky that the English navy had got to him first. If he'd lived, he would have been press-ganged into Parliament, as Miles had been.

He had no patriotic loyalty to the government he was expected to join and even less faith in this antiquated inheritance of power without money. There was to be no magical solution to his previous problems. Instead, everyone expected he would sort out the mess left to him by his distant relatives.

Worse yet, there had been a stack of tear-stained letters from Prudence that had beaten him across the Atlantic on a faster ship. The situation was dire. He was her last and only hope. He must return home to Philadelphia immediately.

But would he be allowed to do so? He did not think that the Prince who was currently running things would drag him back to the House of Lords in leg irons. But after what had happened to Ed, he could not be sure. His brother had gone to Barbados in an attempt to turn the family fortunes by investing in sugar. The next any of them had heard, he'd been impressed into the British navy. In his last letter home, he had begged Miles to watch over Prudence until he could return to her.

Shortly after that Pru had got the news that she was an impoverished widow. And now, the moment Miles was not there to watch her, she had made things worse. She was an exceptionally foolish girl and probably deserved what she got. But she was his responsibility, more so than these English strangers were. She needed him. What could he do but run back to Philadelphia, as fast as he had run from it?

It did not seem likely that Miles could leave from any of the ports around London, without someone noticing. So, he'd left the city making a vague reference to visiting the Comstock property while omitting the rest of his plan, which was to keep going until the entire country was no more than a distant memory.

He'd set off at a gallop and the fine blood he was riding was eager to carry him at full speed. It was the best horse he'd ever sat, much less owned. He'd had no trouble buying it on credit, since earls did not bother using actual money.

He must find a way to return it to its previous owners. In England, peers who could not pay for the things they bought suffered nothing more than embarrassment. But in America, he'd have been hung as a horse thief. His guilt when he looked at the bill to Tattersall's was almost too much to stand.

What did bother him even more than the debts was having strangers scraping and bowing and calling him my Lord Comstock. He wanted to shout, 'You don't know me.' If they did, they would realise that they had made a mistake in thinking a common ancestry qualified him to do the job they had foisted upon him.

After half a day's journey, he passed the marker that indicated the edge of the Comstock holdings. There was no denying that the land he'd inherited was pretty, with rolling farmland and a village full of thatched-roof cottages. The view was spoiled when he paused to realise that he was responsible for keeping those roofs from leaking. But at least the tavern served a decent ale and did not enquire about his past, despite his accent. The last thing he needed was to be identified as their new lord and master before he could finish his drink.

After a light lunch he rode on towards the estate. But as he came around a turn in the gravel drive he saw two houses: the great house on the hill and a second house, large by normal standards, but dwarfed by the manor beyond it.

The smaller one must be the dower house that he'd been told of. It had been described as almost beyond repair, which meant it was unoccupied and unattended. If there was a couch, or at least a dry patch of floor to lay out his bedroll, he might stay there unnoticed. It would save him the trouble of making excuses to the servants at the great house about his sudden arrival and equally sudden departure.

And if there happened to be a set of silver left in a sideboard, he might still see some profit from this unfortunate trip. When pawned, a saddlebag full of second-best decorations would at least be enough to buy a ticket for home.

He dismounted, looped the reins over a nearby tree branch and approached the house. But before he'd got within ten feet of the door he heard a familiar angry bark and felt a fifteen-pound projectile strike his calf.

He stared down at the little black-and-white head, with the equally small fangs sunk ineffectually into his boot leather, and resisted the urge to kick.

Instead, he reached down, grabbed the dog by the scruff of the neck and tugged it free, then lifted it to eye level, glaring at it.

The dog returned the sort of look normally reserved for cats and creditors.

'I do not know what possessed me to rescue you at the docks, since this is all the thanks I've got for it. If this is how you treated your previous owner, I understand why he was trying to drown you.' It had been instinct that made him drop his luggage and grab for the burlap sack that the boy had been trying to fling off the gangplank of the *Mary Beth*, assuming that the child's father had told him, harshly but sensibly, that a sea voyage was no place for a dog. By the time he'd turned to assure the little attempted murderer his pup would be safe, the boy had vanished and Miles had been the owner of the most ungrateful cur in the New World.

'Grrr...' The animal made a snap at the empty air, trying to reach him. Miles had told himself for weeks that the dog's bad temper was caused by close confinement and the constant rocking of the ship. But he appeared to be no happier on the dry land of England than he had been in America.

'When I sent you on ahead with the Dowager, I hoped we might never see each other again. Have you managed to get yourself banished from the main house already?'

The dog squirmed in his hands, taking another snap

before wriggling free and jumping to the ground. Then, he turned towards the dower house and leapt through a broken window, still barking.

Miles sighed. 'I am not climbing in after you. There is a perfectly good door.' He walked to the front of the house, reaching into his pocket for the ring of keys, before noticing that it already stood open a crack.

'You can come out on your own,' he called. 'You have four good legs on you and no longer need my help.' He listened for a scrabbling of paws or any other sign that the dog had heard and meant to obey him. If he planned to stay here, it might be handy to have the little beast chasing down rodents for him. With the door left ajar, the place was probably crawling with them. But since the dog loathed him and tried to bite each chance it got, he was probably safer putting it outside and trying to befriend the rats.

As he stepped into the house, it surprised him that there was no sign of the dog, nor the sound of barking from deeper inside. Was there a chance that it had fallen through a weak floorboard, or injured itself on broken glass? He was a fool to care for a thing that wanted no part of him. But at least there was no one around to witness his softness. He advanced into the house. 'Where are you, you little bastard?' With luck, he could lead it back towards the open door without incurring any damage to boot or hand. Then, he could block the window and lock the door against it until it gave up harassing him and found its way back to wherever it was being kept.

Miles looked around him at the entryway to the

dower house. Except for the dog, the place would not be a bad one to hole up in, until he decided what to do with himself. The Dowager had spoken of repairs too expensive to render the place liveable. But she was a great lady, used to comfort and entertaining. To a man used to sleeping rough, it was near to a castle. It was damp, of course. But a fire would help that. And the furniture had been covered to protect it against time and the elements, which would likely enter through the leaks in the roof. He would not trust the mattresses to be dry, but in the rooms he passed on the way to the dog, there were no end of tables and chairs, and probably a few long benches and sofas that would make a decent bed if one was tired enough. It would do nicely, even if he couldn't find any silver worth selling.

A streak of black-and-white fur passed by the doorway ahead of him. There was another familiar bark as the dog came to the end of whatever course it had set for itself. Then a moment's pause before it pelted back across the opening in the opposite direction. The creature had played a similar game on the ship, running back and forth down the companionway, dodging curses and kicks from angry sailors and passengers before racing back into his cabin and falling into an exhausted heap at the end of his bunk.

It had been amusing the first time. Now it was just annoying. But before he could shout at it, someone else said, 'Pepper! Be still.'

He froze. Though it had the strength of a general, the voice was definitely female. Was it the empty house that gave it such an unusual tone? It seemed to echo, yet was strangely muffled. He approached the room in front of him with caution, not sure if it was better to confront her, or sneak away unnoticed.

When he passed the threshold, the explanation was obvious. The dog had halted his insane racing and was sitting on the hearth, sniffing at the pair of women's boots standing on the andirons. As he watched, one of them lifted as the woman wearing them stretched her body upwards, reaching for something in the chimney.

There was a shower of soot and a muffled 'Damnation.'

The dog retreated with a sneeze, waiting for the ash to settle. Then, as helpful as ever, he lurched forward and grabbed a mouthful of skirts, swinging on them to further unbalance their wearer.

Miles could not help it. He laughed.

Slowly, the boot lowered, seeking footing on the grate. 'Whoever you are, if you mean to harass me, I have a poker and am not afraid to use it on you.' If her arm held the same resolve that her tone did, any blow delivered would likely be strong enough to make him think twice.

'And I have a pistol,' he countered. 'But I don't think either of us need worry, because neither of us wishes to resort to violence. At least until we know each other better,' he added. In the past, there had been more than one woman ready to crown him with cast iron. As yet he had given this one no reason.

The dog skittered away as the boots hopped off the grate. After some shifting and more falling soot, the rest of the woman appeared in the opening of the fireplace. The rest of the girl, rather. Though she could not have been more than twenty, she was fully, and quite nicely, grown. Her bespectacled face was rather plain, though he doubted the smudges of ash on it helped her appearance. But one would have to be a fool to call a woman with such finely turned ankles homely.

She had nice calves, as well, even under the thick stockings she was wearing. He'd caught a glimpse of them as the dog had tugged at her skirts. And though the sensible gown she wore made no effort to flatter her figure, it could not manage to hide a slim waist and a fine bosom. He was not normally given to debauchery, probably because he had never been able to afford it. But if the village girls in Comstock were all as comely as this one, it might be tempting to play lord of the manor.

As if the dog could sense what he was thinking, its hackles rose and it faced off between him and the girl, baring teeth and offering a warning growl.

Miles braced himself for impact.

'Pepper. Sit.'

As if by miracle, the dog responded to her command and dropped to its tiny haunches, still staring at him.

'If you try anything, I will set my dog on you,' she said, giving him a look as fierce as the terrier's.

'Your dog?' he said, surprised.

She hesitated. 'The Earl's dog, then. But since he is not here and I am a member of his family, Pepper's responsibility and affection have transferred to me.'

He opened his mouth, ready to argue that the owner of the ungrateful cur was right in front of her, should the animal choose to acknowledge him. But since Pepper was incapable of loyalty, obedience, or any other canine virtue, it refused to claim him.

Then he remembered that if his goal had been to slip on to the Comstock property and off again, unnoticed, he should not announce himself to the first person he saw, especially if he had been fortunate enough to meet a family member who did not immediately recognise him.

She was staring at him with narrowed eyes. 'And now that I can look at you, it is apparent that you are not the common tramp I was fearing.' She tipped her head. 'By your accent, you are American. I'd think you were a member of the Earl's party, but I was told he travelled alone.'

'We came on separate ships,' he said, falling easily into the first lie that came to mind. 'I was to arrive first, but the seas were rough.'

'You are the auditor, then,' she said. There was no triumph in her voice, just a flat acknowledgement of the assumed fact.

He nodded, relieved to have his work done for him. But the auditor from America needed a name. 'Potts,' he said, automatically. He must look like the name suited him, for Greg Drake had mistaken him for just such a fellow when they'd met. 'Augustus Potts, at your service, ma'am.' He bowed to hide his wince at the Christian name that had popped into his head. Hopefully, the lie would not be needed for long. Who in their right mind would want to spend any length of time as Augie Potts?

'Mr Potts,' the girl replied, in the tone of one used to ordering servants about.

'And who do I have the honour of addressing?' he said, already suspecting that he knew the truth.

'Miss Charity Strickland. Your employer's distant cousin.'

He nodded in acknowledgement. He'd met her sister Hope, already. With some effort, he could see a resemblance. They shared the same wide brow and pointed chin.

But where Hope was uncommonly pretty, Charity was not currently so blessed. There was something too grave in her expression and the look in her eye was too discerning for one so young. Though she was not a lovely girl, he suspected she would age into her beauty and become a rather handsome woman.

'Were you sent to inventory the main house?' she said, in a matter-of-fact way to remind him that it was not his job to be standing here, staring at her.

'And the dower house, as well,' he said.

'There is nothing of value here.'

In a pig's eye. Her response had been a trifle too quick and too specific for his taste. She had come here to retrieve something or to hide it. And people did not normally take the time to hide things that were worthless. 'If the house is empty, it makes me wonder what you were doing here, halfway up the chimney.' He gave her a subservient smile. 'Is there something I can assist you with?'

'Birds have been coming down it and into the house. I was attempting to close the flue.'

'I see.' That was an even bigger lie than her last words had been. But if he was claiming to be Augie Potts, he could hardly point fingers. Instead, he stripped off his coat and rolled up his sleeves. 'Give me the poker, then. My arms are longer.'

'That is all right,' she said hurriedly.

She was far too eager to handle the matter herself. 'Then, at least let me go up to the house and find a footman. A member of the family should not be doing servants' work.'

'That will not be necessary,' she said, not bothering to try to charm him with a smile. 'I think I have managed the matter well enough.'

He raised an eyebrow. 'I did not interrupt you before you could complete what you were attempting?'

Her lips tightened ever so slightly with annoyance. 'Certainly not.'

'Then, allow me to give you a ride back to the main house.'

'That will not be necessary, either,' she snapped.

'But we are both going the same way,' he reminded her. 'Since I have never been to the manor, I would appreciate a guide.'

'It is not possible to get lost,' she said. 'The house is barely a mile away and you are on the drive already.'

She was trying to get rid of him. He had no reason to care why, for he was as eager to be gone as she was to have him so. Yet for some reason, he could not resist annoying her. 'That is likely true. But it would be helpful if you could introduce me to the rest of the staff.' He glanced out the window. 'And a storm seems to be gathering. It has grown darker as we have been talking. I would not want to leave you here in the rain.'

'I can wait inside until it passes,' she countered.

So she had not finished what she had come to do. Since there was nothing in her hands, it seemed likely that she was searching for something rather than secreting something she'd brought with her. In either case, there must be some hidey-hole in the bricks worth investigating, once he had got her safely out of the way.

He smiled at her. 'I am sure the Earl would have my head if I left you here in the rain.' Then he stepped to the room's doorway and waited for her exasperated huff of defeat.

It did not come. Other than a slight narrowing of her eyes, she gave no sign that his attempts to thwart her were annoying her. 'If the Earl wishes it, then very well, Mr Potts. I would never go against his wishes.'

Then she walked past him towards the front door, the terrier following obediently at her heels.

Chapter Two

Charity Strickland's day was not going to plan.

It had been bad enough to climb into the chimney and realise the niche she was looking for was just out of reach. To be discovered doing so had been even worse. Mr Potts was proving to be annoyingly clever, giving no indication that he believed her story about an open flue. He had pretended to, of course. But she suspected he was only toying with her, hoping to worm some piece of information out of her that could be reported to his master.

So far, it appeared that the new Earl meant to do just as she hoped he would, remain in London to perform his duties in Parliament. Should he suddenly decide to take an interest in her welfare, there was no telling what he might consider suitable for her future.

Whatever it was, she doubted it had anything to do with what she preferred for herself. As the youngest of three sisters, she was fed up with being dictated to by people who assumed they knew what was best for her. It had taken months to get the rest of the family out of the way so she might have peace to work. The last thing she needed was a stranger asserting his God-given right to control her because his fortunate birth had made him head of the family.

The season did not end until July and it was barely March. It would take only a few more weeks to accomplish her own plan. If the new Earl of Comstock kept to the business of governing, as he ought to do, she'd be gone long before he arrived, with enough money to set herself up for life in a manner that suited her.

But Mr Potts might prove to be just as annoying as the man who'd hired him. Though he had no right to order her around, so far he was proving to be a first-rate sneak. One had only to look at the dog's reaction to him to know that he was not to be trusted. Pepper's hackles had been raised from the moment that the auditor arrived. As they left the dower house, he was dancing along between them, biting at the man's boot heels as if hoping to scare him away.

To Mr Pott's credit, he had not given in to impulse and kicked at the dog. Perhaps he was not irredeemable. Or perhaps he had better sense than to abuse a pet belonging to a peer in full sight of a member of the family.

When they arrived at his horse, he stepped clear of the little black and white dog and mounted, offering a hand to her to help her into the saddle in front of him.

She smiled at him, wishing for not the first time that she'd inherited any of her sisters' natural charm.

'I could not possibly go without Pepper. I would not want him to become lost.'

Potts looked down at the little dog with obvious disgust. 'In my experience, animals like this are surprisingly hard to lose.'

'But what if this time is the exception? He might be set upon by some wild beast.'

'You have wolves roaming so close to the house?'

'No,' she admitted.

'And I am told there are no bears left in England. What else can there be?'

'A hawk. Or perhaps an eagle.'

He sighed. 'Next you will be telling me England has daylight owls.' He held out a hand. 'Give him to me.'

She scooped the dog up and offered him.

Potts took him by the scruff of the neck, nimbly dodging the snapping jaws and dropped him into the leather bag at the side of his saddle. The dog disappeared for a moment, like a swimmer beneath a wave. Then his head poked out from under the flap, offering something that looked rather like a canine grin.

'There.' Potts held out a hand. 'And now, you.'

Gingerly, she offered her own hand and he pulled her up. He seemed to exert no strength at all, settling her on to the saddle in front of him, to sit on one hip. Then his arms took the reins on either side of her waist, holding her in place as they set off.

Though he showed no signs of noticing it, it was a surprisingly intimate arrangement. Perhaps such behaviour was common in America. Or perhaps she was not pretty enough to move him. He handled the horse as easily as if he was riding alone.

But for her, it was strangely disquieting. Though she did not normally dwell on the appearances of the men around her, it was hard not to notice this one. The arms that wrapped around her were long, as were the legs that brushed against her skirts. He must be well over six feet. He was not precisely gaunt, but there was an angular quality about his frame that seemed to carry to his face. The planes of his cheeks were sharp, as was the line of his jaw. His pale skin might have given another man an aristocratic air, but on him it seemed more scholarly than aloof, as if his studies kept him from the sun.

This attracted her more than his fine features or the shock of dark hair shading his brow. He looked like someone who might be content to hole up in a library. Though the muscles she could feel in the limbs surrounding her did not come from inactivity, he looked like a kindred spirit.

But it did not really matter what he looked like, or how he had come to be so. Men, especially ones that looked the way this one did, never gave such scrutiny to her. She turned her head and looked resolutely forward at the house they were approaching.

'Comstock Manor,' he said, stating the obvious. But there was a tone beneath the words that sounded not so much impressed as stunned.

'You did not think it would be so large,' she said.

'I was told. But I could not believe it was true.'

'It represents everything that is wrong with the family,' she said. 'Something that started as a good idea but grew out of hand until it was no longer possible to manage or afford.'

'No wonder there has been trouble finding someone to record the contents. Who would want to take on such a job?'

'We have lost more valuables than most people own,' she said, speaking quite close to the truth. 'Though most of them are not actually gone. They are just sitting in one of the forty rooms, waiting to be rediscovered.'

She felt something quicken in him at the mention of this surplus of material wealth, a faint, covetous quivering of his nerves. Then he relaxed again, as if afraid that she might have noticed his interest. 'As a member of the family, I would think that you would be in a position to know where some of those things are.'

'I might be,' she said, turning back to blink at him in what she hoped was an innocent way. 'The Earl will never be able to have an accurate accounting of them if I do not help. And I doubt you will be able to learn the lay of the place in whatever time he has allotted for the job.'

The horse pulled up short.

'How would I…? I mean, you are right that there is no way for me to do this job without help. But the Earl would not know one way or the other, if I got it wrong, would he?'

He had not even crossed the threshold and he was already giving up. Or did he mean to collect full pay for a slapdash job? His reasons did not matter. Carelessness, laziness or moral flexibility would all suit equally well as a reason for his departure.

'He will not know if the inventory is not complete unless we tell him,' she said, choosing her words carefully. 'But I have no intention of spreading tales to a man I never met, just because other men I have never met decided he is the heir.'

'I see,' he said, in an equally careful tone.

'I am sure he is depending on your friendship for an accurate accounting,' she added.

'My friendship.' Mr Potts laughed. 'I can tell you in all truth that six months ago, I knew nothing of Comstock, his title or his property.'

This was even more interesting. If the Earl had hired a stranger to see to his interests abroad, he was likely to get the results he deserved. 'The property is not technically his,' she reminded him. 'It belongs to the Crown.' She smiled again. 'But, as an American, you have no real loyalty there, do you?' She had opened the door to conspiracy. Now they would see if Mr Potts walked through it.

'Loyalty?' He laughed again. 'The whole point of my country was to escape this one. And yet, here I am, surrounded by riches that do not belong to the Earl and debts that do.'

'That is a pity,' she said with a shake of her head. 'In my opinion, the task set for you is a hopeless one. If you chose to resign from it, you could be long gone from here before anyone noticed your absence.'

Behind her, he started in surprise. 'Miss Strickland, I was thinking just such a thing when you arrived.' His eyes narrowed. 'But then, I would not be paid, would I? And an urgent need for funds was the only reason I even considered the job.'

Then she made the most daring move at all. 'The house is not lacking for ornaments. If you chose to take something to compensate for your lost time, who would know?'

There was a long pause as he considered her words. But just as she was sure he would succumb, he baulked. 'Stealing from the Earl would be wrong. Both a breach of the Commandments and the law.'

'Of course,' she added hurriedly, annoyed. If morality was seriously a concern, she might never get rid of the man. The next temptation would have to be far more subtle. 'But there is no need for us to be discussing such things in the middle of the drive. As you said before, a storm is approaching. Come into the house and we will get you settled.'

And then she could go to work on him. Once he had seen the house and his place in it, he might be gone by morning.

When his ancestral home had been described to him, Miles had got a vague impression of a large but dilapidated manor in the country. But there was no way he could have imagined the thing that stood before him now. It appeared to be two or three large houses built cheek by jowl, as if the owners could not quite decide what they'd wanted and simply kept building on to it until the money had run out.

Having seen the accounts, that seemed to be exactly

what had happened. When he'd set out from America, he'd assumed that all English lords had to be rich. But his family had run through their money generations ago. The rents from the tenants barely kept pace with the cost of maintaining the property. All that was left beyond them was the house and its contents. And the most valuable items were things he was not supposed to sell. He was expected to hold them in trust for future generations that might never be born if he could not manage to settle his business now.

But the caution to respect the entail had not impressed his ancestors. After greeting him on his arrival, the widow of his predecessor had barely taken a breath before announcing that the diamonds in the Comstock family jewels had been replaced with paste long before she became Countess. The Earls and Countesses of Comstock had been telling lies about their value for so long that it might as well be declared a family tradition.

On hearing this, he had assumed that there was nothing left of value. But though the collection of silver-framed miniatures on the hall table was not enough to save an earl from a life of ruin, the humble Miles Strickland could sell a sack full of them and have enough to live modestly for a good long time.

'What do you think of it?' He had almost forgotten Cousin Charity, who had led him in through the front doors and introduced him to the butler, Chilson, who had signalled for a footman to take his valise and another to remove the snapping dog from the saddle bag.

'I do not know where to begin,' he said, peering

down the hall at what seemed to be an endless line of doorways, then staring back at Charity.

'Do not worry. I will help you.' There was no flirtation in the smile she gave him, only a sly twinkle in her eye that made him think any aid he received would benefit her more than him. Her companionable self-interest was an improvement on recent interactions with the fair sex.

When they realised he had a title, the women of London were friendly to the point of predation. He could hardly blame them for it, since they took their cues from the mamas and papas who were practically throwing their daughters into his path. Even the damned Prince who was currently running the country said that an earl without a countess was not doing his duty. He was supposed to marry, soon and well, for the sake of the title's succession.

Apparently, he was to be bred like livestock. If the activity hadn't involved marriage, he would have been all for it. But since a legitimate child was required, it took much of the fun out of his newfound popularity.

Since this distant cousin didn't know who he was, she was currently treating him with the same indifference as women had before his sudden elevation. But since Charity was also the last unmarried girl in the family, the condition was likely temporary. Once she guessed his identity, she would chase him like a hound after a coon.

'Thank you for the offer of aid,' he replied. 'And I assume this help will be in exchange for everything I can tell you about the new Earl?'

'I think I know all I need to on that front,' she said, with a frown that surprised him. It looked almost like a grimace of distaste.

'Has he done something to put you off?' Miles said.

'He has done nothing so far,' she said. 'That suits me well, but I doubt it will continue. And the last thing I need is for him to arrive on my doorstep with a proposal.'

'Your doorstep?' He glanced around him.

'Metaphorically speaking,' she replied. 'It is technically his house. I plan to be out of it before he arrives. But I am not quite ready to go yet, hence my hope that he will stay in London until Parliament ends its session.'

'And you do not want to marry him,' Miles said, strangely annoyed.

She shrugged. 'It is not logical to expect instant compatibility, based on the convenience of a family connection. It is not as if I believe in something so foolish as the need for romantic love when marrying. But I do not want to rope myself to him or any other man for a lifetime without bothering to learn if we are temperamentally similar.' She glanced down her nose at him, in frank and unladylike appraisal. 'So far, I have not found many available men to my taste. I have exceptionally high standards, Mr Potts.'

He stared back at her, just as rudely, ready to say that plain girls were not usually so particular. Then he remembered her fine ankles and bit his tongue. 'And so you should, Miss Strickland. If you meet him, you will find that the new Earl is not a bad fellow.' Not totally bad, at least. 'But you are right not to expect a marriage from him, sight unseen.'

She smiled at him in earnest now. The brightness of it transformed her face into something that was not beautiful, but held a certain allure that her frowns did not. 'You are the first person to say that to me, Mr Potts. It is quite a novelty to hear such frankness.'

'There is no reason for me to be anything else,' he said, ignoring a stab of guilt. He had not been in any way frank. Worse yet, he had been talking about himself in the third person.

He cleared his throat. 'And now, where would you recommend I begin my search—that is, my inventory?'

'I suggest you begin by settling into your room and washing for dinner,' she said with another shrug and an innocent blink. 'If the accounting of Comstock's possessions has waited for years, there is no reason to begin them this minute. You will find the job less daunting after a good night's sleep and a decent meal.' She walked up the stairs in front of him, casting a look over her shoulder to see if he followed. 'Well?'

He paused. In any other woman, he might have thought it flirtatious, should she lead him straight to his bedchamber. But even on such a brief acquaintance, it was clear that Miss Charity did not flirt.

She likely did not know any better. He started up the stairs after her. 'Surely it is not necessary for you to show me to my room.'

'I shall be showing you a lot more than that before we are done with each other,' she said.

He started in surprise.

Now her look was faintly exasperated. 'You want to know the house, don't you?'

'Well…' He did, of course. But was she really so unaware of him that her words held no hidden meanings at all?

'Then you might as well enjoy the best of it.' At the top of the stairs she marched briskly to the far end of one hall, waving at the corridor behind her. 'The family stays in that wing. Grandmama is at the end, as is the Earl's suite. The corridor to our right leads to the old part of the house. This side is for guests.' She had reached a door at the very end. 'And this is the Tudor room.' She threw open the door and stood in front of it, gesturing inside. 'It is said that Henry Tudor himself stayed here.'

He racked his brain for a moment, to attach significance to the name. 'The King with all the wives.'

'Six,' she said with a deadpan look that announced her opinion of his limited knowledge of local history.

He held up his hands in surrender. 'I can tell you everything you might wish to know about George Washington, if that makes a difference.'

'I can tell you about him, as well,' she said, arching an eyebrow. 'There are books in England, you see.'

'In America, as well.' Damn few of them in his past, of course. But that was no fault of his. He looked ahead at the room in front of him. 'So a king stayed here.'

'And now, you shall.'

He supposed he should be honoured. He rarely cared about the previous occupants of the room, as long as the bed was soft and the sheets were clean. This would be luxurious, though not quite as good as the master suite he was entitled to. But he could hardly ask for that. Then he stopped to wonder. 'Why would you give an auditor the best room in the house?'

By the time he'd turned to hear her response, her face was pleasant, passive and hospitable. But before that, had he seen a flash of something else? Alarm, perhaps?

If so, it was gone and she appeared to be the perfect hostess. 'I want you to be happy. You are the Earl's friend, after all. I can hardly treat you like staff.'

He glanced into the room, filled with any number of items worth taking when he went on his way. 'How very kind of you, Miss Strickland.'

She gave a concluding nod. 'Now, I will leave you to refresh yourself. Dinner is in the dining room at eight, Mr Potts. Do not be late.'

He hesitated for a moment, at the sound of the unfamiliar name, before getting his story straight and responding with an equally polite nod. 'As you wish, Miss Strickland.'

Then she was gone down the hall, leaving him alone in the bedchamber of a dead king. He shut the door quietly behind her and turned to the matter at hand, his private appraisal of the room's worth. What was there in this room that was worth selling? The furniture was valuable, the canopied bed hung with slightly dusty velvet on brass rings as thick as his thumb. Interesting, but not worth the effort of dragging down the drapery. The crossed swords over the mantelpiece gave the room a distinctly masculine air. If they were a relic of the room's namesake they might be priceless. But to get them away he'd have to march through the entire house with a sword on his shoulder. The bedchamber he occupied was as far from the front door as it was possible to get.

His train of thought ground to a halt, then circled back, trying to think why that statement seemed so important. She'd said she'd put him in this room because of his supposed friendship to the Earl. But he had just told her that he had no real acquaintance with Comstock. Had she forgotten?

There was something about Miss Strickland that made him think she did not often lose track of the details. Which meant she'd simply told the first lie that had come to mind to explain her choice. There was something strange going on and he meant to find out what it was.

Chapter Three

Once she had put Mr Potts in his room and Pepper in her own, Charity headed back down the main stairs and out the front door, hurrying down the drive towards the dower house. He had been right. It was about to rain. The clouds had darkened considerably since their departure from the house, an hour ago. As she ran the last steps down the drive towards the front door, she felt the first drops striking the hood of her cloak.

She ignored them. She was so close to the truth that she could not let a little weather prevent her from finishing what she'd begun when he'd interrupted her. Of course, she needed an umbrella more than a ladder. She had been able to feel the edge of the niche when she had stood on the grate, but had not been able to reach the depth of it.

But with the arrival of an auditor, the day of reckoning had come and there was not a minute to spare for further preparation. She would find a stool in the kitchen of the other house and make do. Either the box was there, or it was not. She had to know.

She pushed through the dower-house door and slammed it behind her, allowing herself a moment of unfeminine pique now that there was no one around to hear. Then, she hurried to the sitting room, where the chimney was.

'I was beginning to wonder if you were coming.'

Charity gasped and clutched the door frame, startled out of her breath at the words. Mr Potts had removed the holland covers from one of the chairs by the hearth and was sitting comfortably, his long legs stretched out before him.

It took a moment to think of an appropriate response. The cold, rational part of her brain, the part that she could not seem to keep silent, commented that it was rare to be at a loss for words. Or at a loss for breath. It was rare that she was surprised at all. She was accustomed to outthinking the people around her with ease. Yet this stranger had bested her on her home turf.

'You seem to be winded.' He leaned forward and pulled the cover off the chair opposite him with a flick of his wrist. 'Why don't you sit, as well.' Then, he smiled. 'Perhaps I should light a fire for us to chase away the damp of the room.'

He was expecting her to cry out *No!* and confirm his suspicions that there was something up the chimney. She had no intention of obliging him. 'How did you know I would come here? And how did you arrive before I did?'

'What other reason would you have for putting me in a room that faced the back of the house and not the drive?' He held up a hand. 'Do not tell me it is because

I am an honoured guest. I got the distinct impression before that you wished I would go to perdition.'

'Not to hell. Just back to America. Or London, at least. Even after much preparation, the house is in a frightful state and not ready to be inventoried.' She smiled and fiddled with her glasses, doing her best to appear young and out of her depth. 'My sisters are both just married and Grandmama is travelling on the Continent. It is only just me now.'

'But none of that explains why you would put me in the best room in the house,' he said. 'I assumed you wanted to finish what you were doing without my noticing your departure from the house. You did not come all the way here to close a flue. You were searching for something.'

She touched her hand to her chest, feigning outrage. 'What reason would I have to lie about such a thing?'

'I have no idea,' he replied. 'But I wanted to find out. It would have been impolite to ask you. It is one thing to accuse a woman you've just met of lying and quite another to catch her in said lie.' He stretched his arms, lacing his fingers and cracking his knuckles. 'So I shimmied down the drainpipe running beside the window of my room and came back here to see if you would return.'

'If I hadn't?'

'Then I'd have said nothing more of my suspicions.'

Her heart was still beating faster than normal, probably from the shock he had given her when she'd come into the room. And once again, the rational voice spoke in her mind. Or rather, it laughed derisively. Now she was unsure what she should say next. It was a new feeling to be unsure of herself. She did not think she liked it.

But he seemed to be enjoying it immensely. 'It will save us both some time if you simply admit that I am right. Then I will help you look for whatever it is you are hunting for and we can return to the main house.'

'I might not be searching for anything,' she said. 'I might have been hiding something.'

'I interrupted you before you could complete what you were doing. You had nothing in your hand when you came out of the chimney and I felt no bulges in your skirt that might indicate you'd concealed an item in your pocket. And the minute you could get rid of me, you came back to finish your search. It is far more likely you were looking for something than leaving something.'

His logic was not perfect, but it was better than she usually encountered. And he had let slip something far more important than a demonstration of deductive reasoning. He had all but announced that, while they had been riding, he had not just been supporting her to keep her from falling. He had held her tight enough to discern the contents of her pockets. Her heart was thumping in her chest, both from the memory of his hands on her and the subtlety of his reason for it.

He had searched her. And she had let him to it, behaving like a foolish school girl, excited to be in the arms of a handsome man. If she was not careful, he would run her like a greyhound after a hare, destroying her plans for an independent future. She must be much more careful.

'Suppose you are correct in your assumptions,' she

said. 'Why would you offer to help me?' She watched for a slight change in expression that might tell her what he was really thinking.

'I assume that what you are seeking is a part of the estate. We both want it to be found and returned. Don't we?' He steepled his fingers and stared at her as though daring her to deny it.

She should lie and tell him that, of course, that was what she'd been doing. To tell the truth was to surrender before he had a chance to attack. If he had the slightest inkling of what was in the chimney, he'd have the whole works under lock and key before she could save even the smallest portion for herself.

'If there is something missing from the entail, it is only right that it should be returned,' she said, choosing the hypothetical middle ground, watching for his reaction.

'Or, I could help you find the thing you are looking for and look the other way,' he added, his expression pleasant but opaque. 'I could decide that it was none of my business.' Now he was the one waiting for her response.

She gave the one that most suited the situation and pretended to be shocked. 'Why would you do such a thing?'

'For compensation, of course. It is time for us to lay our cards on the table, Miss Strickland. Whatever you are doing here, I suspect it is something you shouldn't. I will keep your secret, if you pay me to do so.'

'You will keep my secret for now,' she corrected.

'Until you decide I have not paid you enough and come back for more. That is how blackmail works, is it not?'

He laughed. 'Very true.' Then he said, in a conspiratorial whisper, 'I am new at it and have not had the time to think through all the ramifications.'

'Then how about this one,' she said. 'I run back to the house and announce that the auditor is threatening me and I do not think he is an honest man. The servants believe me and contact the Earl. Since he barely knows you, he takes the word of family over anything you might say and fires you immediately.'

Mr Potts gave a brief start of surprise, then clapped his hands. 'Bravo, Miss Charity. Bravo.'

He should be calling her Miss Strickland. Though as he had been patting her hips before, he probably thought he was entitled to some familiarity. 'I did not give you permission to use my Christian name, Potts,' she said, dropping the honorific from his to remind him he was little better than a servant.

He gave an apologetic incline of his head. 'My apologies, Miss Strickland. But my rudeness aside, we seem to have arrived at an impasse. What are we to do?' Then he looked at her for the answer.

She considered. It did not really matter if he was a paragon of virtue, or a total villain. The typical masculine response to a situation like this was usually much the same: to go to the chimney and take what was in it. She was smaller and weaker, and she could not stop him. But Potts was confusing her. He was tailoring his actions to hers and at least pretending that she could decide what would happen next.

To flatter your pride, announced the voice in her head. *This one is a charmer. Be on your guard.*

She touched her finger to her chin, pretending indecision, and scuffed the floor with the toe of her boot. Then she stared at him and spoke without irony. '*We* are going to allow me to get on with what I was doing, Potts. It may still amount to nothing. But if I do not do what I came here for, you will do it yourself as soon as my back is turned and abscond with anything you find.'

He nodded. 'You have a surprisingly bleak view of my character, Miss Strickland. Not inaccurate, mind you. Simply bleak. But if the thing you are searching for can be split easily between us, I will be out of your hair and your life before cock's crow.'

She clutched at her heart, feigning ecstasy at the thought of his absence. 'Will you really, Potts?'

'My plan on coming here was exactly what you suggested when we first met. I have urgent business back in America and no money for a return passage. I should not have to count every last part of the Comstock entail to get it. If I can find something of value that won't be missed, I will take it, sell it and get a ticket on the first ship bound for Philadelphia.' He pointed to the fireplace. 'If there is such a thing hidden up that chimney, then go to, Miss Strickland. Go to.'

'Very well, Potts,' she said, with another insincere smile. If they found what she was looking for, there was no way he could take half of it, any more than she could. But he had planned to take something that would not be missed. She must hope that he could be steered towards discretion and not greed. Then she remembered that there were other issues to be dealt with. 'I have but one problem. I was too short to reach it on the last visit.'

'I am taller,' he said, standing up, ready to take her place.

'And wider,' she reminded him. 'It was a snug fit, even for me.'

'There is nothing for it then,' he said, went to the fireplace, hauled the grate out of its place and went down on one knee, patting the level plain of his opposite thigh. 'Up you go.'

'I was thinking more of finding a ladder,' she said.

'Have you brought one with you?'

'Do not ask me facetious questions,' she snapped.

He patted his knee again. 'Come along, Miss Strickland. Let us settle the mystery in the chimney and then you will have time to berate me on my character.'

She sighed. She did not need her sisters to tell her that what he had suggested was improper. It would take only a minute or two to find something else to stand on. But she wanted an answer to the mystery, not in two minutes, but *now*.

Everyone said that impatience was a major flaw in her character. And she would address it later.

She stepped forward, crouched to move past him in the fireplace opening, braced herself on the walls of the chimney and raised a foot.

Before she could fumble, he had grabbed her boot and guided it to a place on his thigh. Then he reached beneath her skirts and tapped the back of her other knee as one might do to a horse to make him raise a hoof.

She lifted the foot that was still on the ground and he made a stirrup with his hands, boosting it to join the other one so she could stand on his leg.

He was right. She was several inches higher than she had been when standing on the grate. She felt the bricks surrounding her for the expected niche.

'Anything?' he asked.

'No,' she admitted through gritted teeth. She stretched her fingers upwards and brushed a ridge and empty air where there should be brick, but nothing else. 'I can feel it above me, but I am still too short.'

'Step on to my shoulders, then.' Before she could argue, his fingers were around one of her calves, firmly guiding her leg upwards.

For a moment, her normally agile mind went blank. His head and shoulders were under her skirt. This was the first, and possibly the last, time that a man would see her legs, much less touch them. She must pray that it was dark under there. If he looked up, he would see far more than her legs. He would be inches from everything she had to offer.

It was…

She shepherded her thoughts, trying to analyse the sensations running through her. The feel of his hand on her ankle was different to any touch she'd felt before, though it was not even skin to skin. The flesh under her wool stocking felt cold, but the blood beneath was racing hot, back towards her heart. And above it all, she was sure she felt the gentle stirring of his breath.

The world seemed to spin and waver around her, unsteady, as if she'd had too much wine. Then she realised that the feeling was not imagination. Her body trembled, trying to find balance as he guided it to stand on his shoulders like a Vauxhall Gardens acrobat. She could stop it by bracing herself against the brick walls around her.

She did so. But she didn't like being steady. She wanted to feel strange and unsure, laughing as the whole world dropped from under her and she fell to land breathless in his lap.

'Miss Strickland?' The voice coming from under her skirts was muffled, but unemotional.

'Uhh, yes,' she said, hurriedly feeling for the niche in the wall that was now on a level with her face. Her heart gave another sudden swoop as her fingers encountered a box. 'I have found something.'

'Excellent.' Both hands transferred to her left ankle as he began the delicate process of helping her down. By the time her feet were back on the hearthstones, she had regained control of her senses and could emerge, sooty but fully rational, from the fireplace. Then she held out the thing she had found: a wooden box about eight inches square.

'It is not very large,' he said, staring down at it.

'It does not need to be,' she said, fumbling with the catch. But she had thought it would be bigger than this. She had imagined a rectangular, leather case similar to the one that held the duplicates, with an easily found latch and hinges. But the wood under her fingers was completely smooth. Nor did there seem to be a separate top that could be lifted off. If she had not felt the lightness and heard a faint rattle from within, she'd have assumed that it was a solid block and not a box at all.

'Hand it here for a moment,' he said, fishing in his pocket for a handkerchief. Once he had hold of it, he buffed enthusiastically to remove the accumulated ash and grime. Then he handed it back to her to admire.

She adjusted her spectacles, wiping the grime from them to get a clear look. What had seemed to be plain mahogany was at least three colours of wood, inlaid in elaborate marquetry, no two sides alike. But though it was lovely to look at, the way into it was not more apparent now that it was clean than it had been fresh from the chimney. She stared back at him. 'Do you have a penknife I might borrow?'

'And spoil the fun?'

'I am supposed to enjoy this?' she asked, giving it a frustrated shake.

'You are holding a Chinese puzzle box,' he said patiently. 'Perhaps you are not familiar with them, but I have seen them brought from the Orient by sailors.' He held a hand out for the box.

She hesitated. She had spent half a day up a chimney, rooting around in the dirt. She had run back and forth from the house, twice. All she wanted was a cup of tea and a wash and some sign that this quest was nearing its end. Instead, this clean and poised stranger stood ready to take it away and finish it for her.

She pulled it back. 'Thank you, Potts, but that will not be necessary.'

'I thought we agreed to share,' he said, giving her a smile that could melt the snow off a roof.

She shook the box again, hearing only the faint rattle of the trick marquetry that hid the latches. 'As you can hear, there is nothing inside. And, even if the box is rare enough to be valuable, it will no longer be so if you try to take half.'

'Are you sure it is empty?' he asked with a raised eyebrow. 'Perhaps something you do not wish me to see?'

She shook her head and gave him a pitying smile. 'Even full to the brim, a box this size could not hold very much. If you wish the money to return to America, I am afraid you will have to get it by doing what the Earl expected: an inventory of the entail.'

'Well, I must say, Miss Strickland, what got off to a promising start has been a most disappointing afternoon.'

'That could be said of most afternoons at Comstock Manor,' she said. 'But there is no point in spending any more time here. Let us return to the main house. Dinner at eight, Potts. And tomorrow, we will begin the inventory.'

Chapter Four

If her sisters had been here, they would have known how to handle this.

Charity had never needed their advice before. It might seem immodest to think so, but wisdom usually flowed from her in their direction and not from them to her. Though she was youngest, she was better read and better educated than either of them. In matters that truly mattered, she was better at observing and understanding the world and the people in it. It was how she had known, before either of them, which men they were likely to marry. One had simply to watch dispassionately and draw conclusions from the data collected.

But that was not required at the moment. Tonight, she needed to be a polite and gracious hostess to a male stranger. She had never before had to deal single-handedly with a man in a social setting. On the rare times she had been forced from the house to go through the motions of the London Season, Faith and Hope had been there to chaperon and guide her, preventing a merely uncomfortable situation from turning into a fiasco.

But they were not here tonight and she had never felt so alone in her life.

Her first instinct had been to announce that Mr Potts could have dinner served on a tray in the location of his choosing. She would eat in the library, as she usually did, and go to bed after she had managed to solve the puzzle they had found in the chimney.

Now that she was in her room, she had taken the time to examine it. She'd run her hands over the inlaid wood panels, giving it a shake and weighing it with her hands. There was nothing about the sounds it made to indicate that they came from shifting contents and not the puzzle mechanisms themselves. Perhaps the things she'd hoped to find were packed tight in cotton wool, but she would have expected there to be more weight.

The problem deserved several hours' study in the privacy of the library. But she had announced earlier that dinner was a formal arrangement and that he was expected to attend it. To cancel it and devote herself to solving the puzzle would announce to this interloper just how important a matter it was. When she had thought success was imminent, she'd felt that there was no choice but to accept his help. Instead, she had been given a locked box and a small reprieve. If she could make it through supper, she could plead exhaustion and retire to her room to open the box. There was a chance she might still complete her task without his even knowing.

But it was a slim chance, at best. The auditor was

not like the rest of her family, who had long ago given up trying to understand her. When she had tried to outwit Potts, he had not just been able to keep pace with her, he had got one step ahead.

Perhaps it had been mere luck on his part. She prayed that when she came down to dinner she would find him as easy to gull as the rest of her acquaintance. But the little voice at the back of her mind whispered that her true wish was just the opposite. She wanted him to be just as clever at supper as he had seemed this afternoon. She wanted to spend more time with him, not less.

That alone was reason enough to avoid him. She was not thinking sensibly and it was all his fault. If she was not sure that she could best him in a battle of wits, what other weapons did she have?

At times like these, her sisters could fall back on their looks and flirt their way out of trouble. A flutter of eyelashes, a few shy smiles, and even the smartest of men around them tended to forget whatever it was that had been troubling them.

Charity sighed. Flirting required that she pretend to be someone she was not: sweet, biddable and somewhat in awe of the men around her. Even if she could manage those things, she was not pretty enough to dazzle a gentleman, especially not one that could dazzle in his own right.

Potts was astoundingly good looking for an auditor. The men in her family were handsome enough, in a refined sort of way, with brown hair and eyes. But looking at Potts was a study in the contrast of light and shadow. His eyes were so dark that it was a challenge to see where irises ended and pupils began, but they seemed almost black against his pale skin. And though he had smiled often, she'd got only glimpses of his teeth, which were very white and very straight.

Perhaps it was not that he was smarter than she. Perhaps her wits were slowed by the sight of him. The thought was cheering, but highly unlikely. She had yet to meet a man so handsome that she was rendered stupid in his presence. If anything, her mind had been working even faster than usual, now that he had arrived, gathering all the information it could about the man before deciding on a course of action concerning him. Dinner would be an excellent time to learn more, pretending that her interrogation was nothing more than polite chatter over the meal.

Charity went to the bell pull in the corner of her room and gave the single sharp yank that would summon her maid. Then she sat on the bed to wait, idly scratching the ears of Pepper, who was already sleeping there. No other female in her family had to go the bother of waiting for a servant. Her sister's maids seemed to be always under foot, often one step ahead of their mistresses when it came to choosing the perfect gown for every occasion. But since Charity rarely bothered with her appearance, she had no right to be surprised that the maid was not pressing ribbons and starching petticoats.

After nearly twenty minutes, the door opened a crack and Dill appeared, staring at her mistress in silence.

Charity stared back at the maid, raising an eyebrow expectantly.

'You rang, miss?'

'Yes, Dill. I wish to dress for dinner.'

'You do?'

Surely the request was not so very odd. 'Yes, Dill. That is why I summoned you.'

'You never dress for dinner, miss. Especially not when we are alone.'

'We are not alone,' Charity reminded her. 'The auditor has arrived.'

'And he will be dining with you?'

'Yes, Dill.'

'In the dining room?'

'That is where we dine, Dill.'

'You usually dine in the library,' the maid said, still confused.

'Not tonight, Dill.'

'And servants dine below stairs,' the maid said, stubbornly. 'An auditor is a sort of a servant, isn't it?'

'He, Dill.' The maid had a point. But employees occupied a place between servants and family. The way they were to be treated was likely situational and better decided by Grandmama, who was absent, just like her sisters.

In the end, Charity decided to lie. 'Mr Potts is a friend of the Earl as well as his auditor. He will be eating in the dining room, like a member of the family.'

'Oh.' Dill stared at her for a moment. 'You don't dress for family, either.'

'But I am dressing tonight.'

'Oh.' Dill gave a nod and a grin that announced she had seen Mr Potts and had a theory about Miss Charity's sudden interest in looking her best.

'Grandmama would expect me to treat a representative of the new Earl with proper respect,' Charity added. When the maid did not move from the doorway, Charity cocked her head in the direction of the wardrobe. 'That is why I have summoned you to help me dress.'

'Ah.' The girl ambled towards the gowns and pulled two from their pegs. Both of them were brand new and with décolletage that Charity found slightly intimidating. Dill grinned again. 'How much respect do you want to show 'im?'

Charity took a deep breath, then pointed to the more modest of the two. 'That one. And a shawl, I think.'

Dill shook her head. 'A shawl defeats the purpose. I will have the footmen build up the fire in the dining room. That and some pepper in the soup and you'll be nice and warm.'

'I suppose you are right,' she said with a sigh. Though the dress would make her feel uncomfortably exposed, it was no worse than what the other girls in London were wearing.

Of course, Mr Potts was not from London. America had been settled by Puritans. Perhaps he would be shocked by her. Or perhaps he would see through her ridiculous attempt to behave as other, normal girls did. Then he would laugh and dismiss her entirely. It would be a disaster, just as it had been in London, on those times she had followed her sisters' advice and tried to mix in society.

She sat quietly as Dill worked over her, afraid to look in the mirror, not wanting proof that she looked as awkward as she felt. It was not as if she needed to impress him. He worked for her family and would have to be polite, no matter how she acted. But whether he voiced it or not, he would have an opinion.

She had escaped to the country because she could not abide the critical gazes and snide comments of the marriage mart, where men treated girls and horseflesh much the same. In both cases, they wanted an animal that was attractive, high-spirited. Then they put a bit in the mouth or a ring on the finger so that it could never think for itself again.

'There, miss. All done.' Dill stepped away, her hands falling to her sides, and added without a trace of irony, 'And do not worry so. You will be the prettiest woman in the room.'

'I will be the only woman in the room, Dill,' she said, putting on her glasses and staring at her reflection. The results were…

Passable. She looked as well as she ever did. She was displaying an unusual amount of skin, which men generally liked. But there seemed to be too much. A gown like this required jewels and she had none.

Then a thought hit her and she smiled. 'Dill, go to Grandmama's room and bring back the case with the Comstock diamonds.'

A decent maid might have questioned her right to wear the things, since they were reserved for the use of the Countess. But Dill was merely adequate and did not bat an eye. She simply returned with the box and placed them on the vanity. Then she pulled a set of ear-bobs from their place and hooked them into the ears that had been exposed by Charity's carefully styled hair.

'The necklace, as well, I think,' Charity said, feeling oddly like she was a little girl again, playing dress up with Grandmama's jewellery.

'In for a penny, in for a pound,' Dill answered, draping the heavy chain over her head until the teardrop-shaped lavalier fell in the hollow between her breasts.

It was an excellent choice. But not for the reason her maid thought. It would give Potts something to look at, other than her. With a three-carat stone in front of him, he would have no reason to care whether the woman wearing it was pretty or not.

And there could be no better way to assure the auditor that the entail was intact than to bring the Comstock diamonds out at the first opportunity. Once he had seen it, she could assure him that the rest of the parure was safe and accounted for. This, the most important item to be inventoried, could be checked off his list. And if he noticed that the stones she was wearing were paste?

She would claim to be just as surprised as he was. Either way, she would be able to draw conclusions about his intelligence and observational abilities. It was information she could use against him later.

She felt somewhat more confident about herself now that she had a plan. But it would not make the dinner any easier. Her stomach filled with nervous butterflies as she walked towards the stairs, only to see him coming down the hall on the opposite side of them.

'Miss Strickland,' he called. 'Ahoy! Or perhaps, avast. I am not sure which is more appropriate in this case.' He walked towards her with a cockeyed grin on his face, looking more appealing than she cared to notice.

She smiled back at him. 'Ahoy is meant to call my attention. Avast is a request that I stop. Which did you want?'

His eyes swept her from head to toe, pausing for the briefest of instants to register the presence of the necklace. Then his gaze returned to her face, still smiling. 'Both. I need an escort to the dining room. This house is not precisely a maze, but it is a long jaunt from end to end. I am likely to starve before the meal if left to my own devices.' Then he held his arm out to her, as if he was about to lead her to the dining room.

But not really. At dinners and balls, the men who took her arm were either assigned to the task by some sympathetic hostess or volunteered because they hoped to make a good impression on one of her sisters. As she walked with them, they did not pay attention to her, but glanced over their shoulders to be sure that someone else was observing their gallantry.

But tonight, the man in front of her was focused solely on her, as if she was the prettiest girl in the room, just as Dill had said. Because they were alone. He was looking at her because there was nowhere else to look. There was nothing personal about it.

'Miss Strickland?' Now he was wondering at her hesitation.

'Just thinking,' she said, trying and failing to duplicate the light, flirtatious smile that her sisters used at times like this. But it was all wrong. She could not manage to look empty-headed while claiming to think. And now she could not decide how she was supposed to look, which must make her seem more dim-witted than thoughtful.

If her shifting expression seemed odd to him, he did not indicate it. He simply continued to smile and guided her down the stairs.

Chapter Five

When they arrived in the dining room, Charity Strickland chose a seat halfway down the table and indicated the place opposite that was set for him. It seemed that the staff had ignored her change in rank as the only family member present and put her in her usual place instead of moving her closer to the head of the table. Even when they were not here, empty places had been left for her sisters.

And for him, as well. The head of the table, where the Earl should be seated, had a place setting, but no chair. He could not help a small shiver of dread at the sight of it and the weird, undeserved respect that was offered to a supposed lord and saviour that none of them could recognise even when he was in the house with them.

'My maid promised that a fire would be lit,' she said, mistaking the reason for his shiver.

'I am fine,' he assured her. 'If you are comfortable, do not concern yourself.' He tried not to glance down at the expanse of ivory skin on display above the neckline of her gown, or to look even lower, searching for her body's reaction to the cold room. Perhaps English gentlemen did not have such thoughts, but the crass American that he was thanked God for the superior view afforded a lowly visitor who was placed opposite Miss Charity instead of at the head of the table.

Her long neck had looked ridiculous in the high-collared dress she had worn this afternoon. But in a dinner gown, her exposed throat swept gracefully down to the swell of her fine, full breasts. Though there had been little light beneath her skirts when he had boosted her up the chimney, he had been holding a fine pair of ankles and felt delightfully rounded calves pressed on either side of his head.

And though her hands moved with masculine efficiency as they sliced the lamb on her plate, the fingers were long and tapered to fine, almond-shaped nails.

There was much to enjoy in the young lady that everyone had been insisting he marry, for duty's sake and the good of the Empire. But there was also one thing he did not like at all. Dangling between those perfect breasts was what had to be the crowning glory of family jewels. The excessively large teardrop pendant would have dazzled him, had he not known it was a worthless copy. Now it merely depressed him.

Did she know? he wondered. Of course she did. The truth was supposed to be a secret passed from Earl and Countess to Earl and Countess. The Dowager had blurted it out to him the first time they'd met, then sighed with relief as if she'd transferred a back-breaking burden on to his unsuspecting shoulders.

As the youngest granddaughter, Miss Charity should know absolutely nothing about it. But she struck Miles as the sort of woman who was exceptionally good at ferreting out secrets. Which begged the question as to why she would flaunt it in front of him at the first available moment.

Because she wanted to convince him that nothing was amiss. Despite himself, he smiled. It was a pleasure to be in the company of a female whose actions had purpose.

She smiled back and the effect on her features was transformative. And for a moment, he forgot himself, grinning back, smitten.

Then she looked at him with a gaze as sharp as an eagle's and said, 'So, Mr Potts, tell me about yourself.'

He could feel the smile freezing on his face, as his brain struggled for an answer. At last, he replied, 'There is not much to tell.' It was true. He had not bothered to invent a past to go with his *nom de guerre*, so what could he possibly say?

She set down her knife and steepled her fingers. 'Tell me anyway. I am fascinated.' She did not look totally sincere, but she did look persistent. 'I have never met an American before.'

He breathed a sigh of relief and a silent prayer of thanks for the topic. 'I am from Philadelphia, in the state of Pennsylvania.'

'Where the Earl is from,' she said.

'It was where we met.' That was metaphorically true, at least.

'And what did you do, in Philadelphia?'

'A bit of this and that,' he said, for it was near to the truth.

'Auditing?'

'Never before. But I have a decent hand and feel qualified to take accurate notes on what is right before my eyes,' he said, deliberately staring down at the counterfeit diamond.

His suspicions on her knowledge of the false diamonds was confirmed. As if she feared the topic of conversation was about to turn to the necklace, she lost interest in talking and concentrated on the strawberry compote that had arrived for dessert.

Which meant it was his turn to question her. He speared a berry on the end of his fork and bit into it with relish before asking, 'Have you had a chance to open the puzzle box we discovered this afternoon?'

'It is not your business whether I have or not, Potts,' she said, not bothering with an honorific as if she sought to put him in his place.

'On the contrary. The box and whatever is inside it are likely to be valuable, or else why would they be hidden? If they are part of the entailed property, I must record them.'

'I doubt they are,' she said, smiling sweetly and trying to put him off his guard, again.

It was badly done. She could not expect to command him one moment and play the fool the next. In response, he gave her a firm smile and a sceptical stare. 'I think you had best let me be the judge, Miss Strickland. It is my job, after all.'

'If there is anything of interest inside, you shall be

the first to know,' she said, not even bothering to look sincere.

'So you have not opened it, yet,' he pressed.

'There has been little time to do so,' she snapped, touching her hair. 'These dratted curls take hours.' Then, as if realising that ladies were not supposed to consider it a waste of time to beautify themselves, she shut her mouth in another forced smile.

'They were well worth it,' he assured her. 'The effect is quite charming.' He paused to see if the compliment had registered.

It had not.

He continued. 'Puzzle boxes can be devilishly tricky things. Some have more than forty steps and secret compartments beyond that. I have done several of them. If you should need help…'

'You think I should come to you?' she said, narrowing her eyes in suspicion.

'Who else is there?' He gave an innocent shrug, then held out his hands to show he meant no harm.

'You are shamelessly angling for an invitation,' she said, both exasperated and surprised.

'I love a mystery,' he said.

'Well, I have no intention of involving you with it, no matter how curious you are,' she said with a sigh, tossing her napkin aside and rising from her seat. 'There are some things that are just too private to share with people outside the family. And as I said before, if it involves the entail…'

'You promise to tell me,' he finished her sentence.

'You have my word.'

Since she had lied to him several times already, he held little hope that she would turn over any valuables she found, no matter how much he might need them. He gave her another disarming smile. 'If not cracking open your mysterious box, how are we to pass the evening?'

'We?' Apparently, she had not planned to entertain him after the meal. She had probably hoped to abandon him and work on the puzzle box. If she did, it would leave him free to stuff his pockets with knick-knacks and take to the road.

And it might leave her with a box holding thousands of dollars of loose stones, any one of which might set him up for life.

'We, Miss Strickland,' he repeated. 'Surely you do not mean to leave me all alone on my first night here? What do you normally do for fun in this mausoleum, after the sun has set?'

'I enjoy a good game of chess,' she admitted, through gritted teeth.

'An excellent suggestion.' In fact, it was almost too good to be true. 'I like nothing better. I will spot you three pieces of your choice.'

'You will what?' she said, narrowing her eyes.

'It is called a handicap,' he said, with excessive patience. 'It gives a weaker player a chance to win.'

Apparently, she did not think she needed one for he could see fury rising in her like water about to boil over a kettle.

'I know what a handicap is, Potts. I have never needed one before and I do not mean to start tonight.'

'Are you sure?' he said, giving her a chance to change her mind.

'I have been the best chess player in this county since I was thirteen,' she said, glaring at him. Then she batted her eyes as if she was some simple female. 'But by all means give my feeble feminine brain the advantage of three pieces. If you can manage a draw, I will let you help me with the puzzle box you are so eager to see inside of.'

'Really?' The secret to her character revealed itself, before he could even suggest the wager. Flattery might get him nowhere. But if he dared to condescend to her, she would not just hand him the keys to the kingdom, she would throw them with all her might.

'Really,' she said, her smile replaced by a determined nod.

'Fair enough,' he said and let the lamb lead him to the slaughterhouse.

The last time Charity had played chess, it had been with Mr Drake, who had been waiting for the opportunity to sneak into Hope's room. He had been so distracted by the thought of her sister it had taken considerable effort on her part to make him feel that he had a chance to win. There was no fun in blunting her play and throwing games to weaker players. But she had not had the heart to punish that poor man when he was already having a difficult time winning Hope.

Tonight would be different. The exceptionally arrogant Mr Potts deserved no mercy. She would take his three pieces. And then she would take the rest, as quickly and painfully as possible.

She set up the game and glanced at his side for only a moment before removing his queen and both bishops from the board.

'Ho-ho,' he said, clapping his hands in approval. 'You mean to make me work for my reward. Very well, then. Let's begin.'

She had underestimated him. After so many years of people doing the same to her, she should have known better. Potts was a cautious player, but relentless, taking her pieces one by one and dodging the traps she set for him, even without the help of his stronger pieces. When she managed to claim a piece, it usually came with the sacrifice of one of her own. And, indignity of indignities, when he took her king, it was done with a clever arrangement of pawns.

She stared at the table in amazement. 'I have never played a game like that before.'

'Then you have led an exceptionally sheltered life, Miss Strickland.'

While that was quite true, it had nothing to do with her abilities at the chessboard. Nor had it anything to do with the quality of his play, which had been masterful.

Now he was staring at her expectantly. And for the first time in her life, she felt in awe of a man and at a loss for words.

'Well?' he said, with an encouraging tip of his head. When she did not respond, he added, 'Have you forgotten our bet?'

She found her tongue again, clearing her throat and

saying gruffly, 'It can hardly be called a bet. You offered me no reward, if you lost.'

'Since I did not lose, that is immaterial.' He gave her a pitying smile. 'Perhaps it would have been kinder of me if I had been more specific when you asked what I did, while in America.' He cocked his head to the side, as if reliving the conversation in his mind. 'I told you a bit of this and a bit of that. But when I was between this and that, and low on funds, I played chess for money.'

And she had fallen right into his hands.

'Before we played, you promised that I could aid you with the puzzle box. May I see it, please?' He was still smiling. Still maddeningly polite.

'Of course,' she said, rising and leading him from the room.

Chapter Six

If nothing else, he had found a way to stop Charity Strickland from questioning him about his non-existent past. Since her loss at the chessboard, she had barely spoken to him and put up almost no fight when he had requested a chance to see the contents of the box.

If it had been another woman, he might have feared that this was a sign of impending storm. But he sensed nothing from this one that hinted at petty tantrums or poor sportsmanship. Though she was clearly not accustomed to it, she responded to the trouncing he had given her with the sangfroid of an English gentleman.

It was rather confusing.

Perhaps it had unhinged her mind. That was why she showed no sign of modesty as she led him to her bedroom, instead of bringing the box to the parlour. Once there, she walked into the room without a second thought, took up the puzzle from her dressing table and sat on the edge of the bed, holding it out to him and gesturing that he join her.

He paused in the doorway, tempted to explain to

her that the situation was totally inappropriate. Even Pepper knew it was wrong, for the detestable little cur looked up from where he had been napping on the pillow and gave a threatening growl.

Charity gave a single snap of her fingers and pointed to a chair on the opposite side of the room.

The dog stood, gave an apologetic wag of his tail, then obeyed, giving Miles a half-hearted glare as he passed.

That left him with no reason to refuse her, other than good manners and common sense. There was also the chance that, if he waited too long, the effect of the chess game might wear off and she would remember that she did not want his help. So he smiled, walked into the room and sat down beside her as if there was nothing odd about it.

She barely seemed to notice him, turning the box over in her hands, caressing the wood and feeling for loose panels and trim. A few moments passed. Then she smiled as the bottom panel slid a half an inch to the left. 'I had no time to examine it before supper. It does not seem so very difficult.' She handed it to him, to find the next step.

'Perhaps not,' he replied, running his fingers along the side before finding the wooden latch that had been exposed and pulling it up with his thumbnail. 'But you agreed to my terms when we sat down to play chess.' He handed it back to her.

'But it does not take a genius, does it?' she said, pivoting the front panel to reveal a keyhole and added, 'Even if that is what you are.'

It was delivered as a statement rather than a compliment and he saw no reason to deny it. 'Perhaps I am. But intelligence does little good for the individual when the people in power are foolish.' For example, when one discovered that one's family had already done irreparable damage to the inheritance. He glanced down at her. 'I suspect you are familiar with that feeling, are you not?' She must be. It was her family, as well. He worked a fingernail into the left side panel until he heard a click.

She opened the little door he'd unlatched and admired the tracery of inlaid metal revealed before prying a bit of it loose and fitting it into the keyhole. 'It is worse for women,' she said. 'Men do not like it when we are too clever. They especially do not like being corrected when they are wrong.' Her forehead creased as she turned the key and heard another click as the top panel popped up to reveal a second, seemingly blank surface beneath.

Despite the small success, she continued to frown and cast a quick look in his direction, as if wondering if she would be expected to apologise for her abilities should she find the solutions faster than he did.

Someone had taken great pains to put her in her place. He suspected that it was the last Comstock, since she had made a point of remarking on jealous men. Until recently, there had been none of them in her family but her grandfather, the Earl. But if today was any indication, the old man had failed to break her spirit.

'My father was the same way, when I was young,' he said, watching her reaction as he took the box and pressed down on the smooth panel until it lifted a fraction of an inch, then gave it back. 'He was quick to cut a switch to correct me when I was wrong, which he defined as being out of agreement with him. But a smart man would have left his sons more than debt when he died.'

'Young ladies are not corrected with physical punishment,' she said softly, staring at the box in her hands. The silence that followed her words made him suspect that it had not been necessary to strike her to leave a scar.

'All his beatings managed to teach me was what sort of man I did not want to be when I grew up. As for my opinion on clever young ladies?' He gave her an encouraging smile. 'If you think I am in error, do not spare my feelings over it. There is nothing worse than being allowed to blunder on in the wrong direction when there is someone right at hand that could set me straight.'

Their conversation appeared to have affected her for she fumbled with the box, unable to complete the next move. She held it out to him with a pleading look, asking for rescue.

He shook his head, smiled and waited.

Encouraged, she took a breath, applied herself and had figured it out in a moment's time, sliding the sides away and lifting out a smaller box, hidden inside the first one.

'Bravo,' he said, clapping his hands. 'Now open it and show me what we have found.'

Some time during the course of the evening she had

lost the guarded manner she'd had at dinner. She did not hesitate or try to shield the truth from him as she undid the last latch.

He held his breath as she slowly lifted the lid to reveal…

'Nothing?' She turned it upside down and shook it, then tapped the sides, searching for another trick.

She passed it to him and he did the same and found nothing. 'Some sort of family joke, perhaps?'

She frowned. 'If so, it is not funny.'

'What is it that you were hoping to find?' he asked, though he was sure he knew.

'Nothing,' she said, shaking her head. 'Nothing at all.'

He had known her less than a day. She had no reason to trust him. But the lie annoyed him more than it should have. He picked up the pieces of the box, fitting them back together, sliding panels and latching latches until it was back as it had been, when they'd found it. 'Then, congratulations, Miss Strickland. If you were searching for nothing, you seem to have found it. And now, if you will excuse me, I must retire. The audit will begin tomorrow and we must hope that it is more productive than tonight.'

Chapter Seven

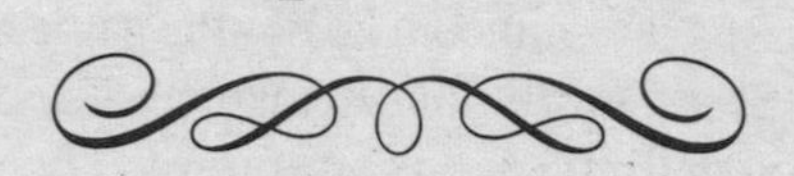

When Charity bothered to imagine her future, it had always included marriage. Though her sisters feared that her lack of interest in society indicated that she meant to remain a spinster by choice, it had never been her intent to spend her life sequestered in the solitude of the family library. She wanted a husband and children and a home of her own, just as her sisters did.

Judging by the besotted way they looked at their husbands, Charity suspected she would be an aunt by the end of the year. The loneliness that had begun creeping into her life since their absence increased at the thought of dandling someone else's baby on her knee. It reinforced her desire for a husband of her own and the children he was likely to give her.

But because something was wanted, that did not mean it would be easy to get. As the years passed, and her sisters grew ever lovelier, Charity had grown more plain. She had only to look in the mirror to realise that it was unlikely that the suitors she might have would be of the handsome and dashing variety.

There were probably any number of quiet, scholarly, not particularly attractive gentlemen that might do. Since such men enjoyed libraries far more than ballrooms, they were surprisingly elusive. When she'd happened upon them thus far, they thought themselves so intelligent that they deserved a wife who would listen more than she talked. She had not expected that they would be even more averse to outspoken women than her grandfather had been.

It was clear that something would be needed to sweeten the pot. Since there was no dowry to be had from the Comstock fortunes, she would have to find one for herself. Thus, she had begun her search for the missing diamonds and the plan to keep just enough of them to make herself attractive to men more poor than particular.

But none of her plans had ever included falling in love. Though her sisters might be convinced that they had married for love, Charity was not even sure the emotion existed in the sense that most girls understood it. She loved her sisters, of course. And her grandmother. She had even loved her grandfather in some hard-to-define way.

But to expect some grand, lifelong passion from marriage was far too impractical. Contentment would be sufficient. She sought a companionable union with a like-minded gentleman who would allow her autonomy in the running of the household and a decently stocked bookshelf. In exchange, she would make no real demands on her husband, allowing him to come and go as he pleased free of tantrums, megrims and excessive millinery bills.

Thus, when love came to Charity Strickland, it struck like an ambush from behind. One minute, she had been slightly annoyed at the condescension of her attractive visitor in thinking that he could best her at a game she knew well. Then, they had begun to play and she'd realised that Augustus Potts was the man of her dreams.

He had lulled her into a false security with a two-knights defence, which was just the sort of primitive, aggressive move that a man might rely on. But once he'd recognised her skill, his game had grown increasingly subtle to accommodate her. While she had initially thought his offer of a handicap was an insult, she learned that it was an attempt to keep the game fair. He'd shown no mercy, simply because she was a female.

By the time he'd put her in check, her pulse had fluttered with excitement. And when he'd declared 'mate in three moves', she had been ready to hand him her heart, as well.

Being in love with Potts had been the worst ten minutes of her life. Why did the object of her adoration have to be a god walking the earth and not an average man who might return her feelings? Why couldn't he at least be willing to stay in England? Why must she break her heart over someone who was brilliant, beautiful and totally unattainable?

Then she had realised that the questions were, in

fact, the answer. She did not love him because he was perfect. She did not love him at all. What she felt was lust. To desire a man like Potts was not just normal, it was sensible. If she was longing to be seduced, the fact that he did not plan to remain in her life or her country was actually an advantage and not an inconvenience.

One question still remained. What did she intend to do about these new feelings?

It had come as a shock to find herself inviting him not just into her bedroom, but on to her bed, so that they might solve the puzzle box. When Grandmama had taught them the basics of etiquette, she had explained that one never brought a man to one's room as one might a woman. When presented with a nearby bed, men were unable to contain their base urges.

Some men, perhaps, but not this one. Potts had simply given her an odd look and sat down beside her on the mattress, more interested in the puzzle and its contents than he was in her.

So she did something that she had never done in her life. It had taken years of practice to not simply blurt out corrections when she knew better than the people around her. After years of scolding from her sisters and grandmother, she had learned that it was one thing to be the smartest person in the room and quite another to rub the fact in the faces of everyone around her.

But tonight, she had looked at the man sitting next to her on her bed and for the first time in her life she had feigned ignorance. She fumbled with a perfectly obvious clue in the puzzle box, handing it to him to solve, hoping to make him like her better.

Instead of being flattered by her need for help, he had raised an eyebrow and handed it back to her, waiting patiently until she had solved it herself. If she had not already wanted him to the last fibre of her being, she had after that.

His adding that he liked being corrected when wrong was like the straw that broke the camel, or the last shot to sink a battleship. Wanting him in secret would not do. She must find a way to have him, or be had by him, even if only for a night. Action must be taken now, or he would be gone and she would not even have a memory.

She lay awake most of the night, putting her prodigious intelligence to work on a plan of attack that would be more successful than her chess game had been. But even as she had lost it, she had won knowledge of her adversary that could be used to her advantage.

He had played the game to get access to the box, only to learn that it was empty. She had been disappointed, but only mildly so. It had been the last in a long line of clues from letters and journals and diaries, and not the first blind alley she had wandered down. She would backtrack and find her way again.

But if he was eager to help her? She smiled. She could invite him on the treasure hunt, offering him information she had already discovered and discounted. He would be just as consumed by the mystery as she had been and willing to do anything to learn more, even if it meant seducing an innocent virgin to steal her secrets.

She gave an involuntary shudder of delight. If she handled him carefully, he might leave Comstock Manor knowing no more than when he came. And she would have a beautiful memory and the treasure all to herself.

Before going down to breakfast the next morning, she summoned Dill again, perplexing the girl by asking for help two days in a row. The end result was a primrose day gown that Charity had always rejected as being too likely to show the dirt and a hairstyle that was not as elaborate as last evening's curls, but softer than her usual tightly pinned braids.

As an afterthought, Dill gave Pepper a good brushing and tied a yellow ribbon about his neck, saying, 'If he means to follow you everywhere, he should learn to look like a lapdog and not a rat-catcher.'

It was probably a mistake, for the little dog seemed to loathe Potts and the feeling was returned in kind. But as usual, the little dog was staring at her, pathetically eager to follow wherever she went.

Charity stared down at him. 'If I must pretend to be tame, so should you. You may come downstairs with me. But one snap and it is off to the stables for the day.'

Pepper wagged his tail, as if he understood and agreed, but it was more likely an attempt to rearrange his fleas. Then he trotted happily at her side as she went down the stairs to the ground floor.

When she arrived in the breakfast room, she found it empty. There was evidence that Potts had been there before her: a footman was clearing away an empty plate and brushing toast crumbs from the table. She glanced at the mantel clock and saw that it was barely nine. When she touched the empty teacup sitting beside his place it was stone cold.

The servant clearing away guessed her question before she could ask and murmured, 'Half past six, miss. He was done well before seven.'

Without bothering to sit, she helped herself to a rasher of bacon from a covered plate. 'Did he say where he was going, after?'

'To work, miss.'

She chewed thoughtfully. Unless the job was to gather eggs while the chickens still slept, she could not imagine the need to rise before nine to do it. Since he was auditing a property that had been collecting dust for centuries, he had got a ridiculously early start. He must be somewhere in the house, but with forty rooms to account for, she could be searching for hours.

She looked down at the dog sitting patiently at her feet, and tossed him a scrap of bacon for incentive. Then she held out another piece, then pulled it away and offered the rumpled napkin sitting beside his place. 'Find him.'

The dog gave a single, long sniff and ran out into the hall.

Charity helped herself to a bun and followed the sound of his barks.

When she caught up to Pepper, he was outside the closed door of her grandfather's study. She hissed at the dog to distract him from scratching at the woodwork and tossed him his reward. Then she reached for the door handle and paused, unable to bring herself to open it. The Earl had been dead for over two years. There was no rule, written or unwritten, that said the room was out of bounds until Comstock arrived. She had been in the study many times herself, even using it to write letters and read.

But on those occasions, the door had been left wide open.

'Doors are closed for a reason, Charity. If you cannot respect that, we will have to find a way to teach you.'

Perhaps that was true. But there was no reason for this one to be closed today. Before she could question the action, she grabbed the handle and yanked it open.

Potts sat in the Earl's chair, his feet up on the desk, reading her grandfather's appointment book. At the sound of the opening door, he looked up slowly and smiled, but made no move to adjust his posture.

For a moment, the sight of a man in that chair at all froze her to immobility on the doorstep. There had been too many arguments here, so many lectures and punishments that she could see a worn spot on the carpet where she stood to receive them. Her fear of the room had dwindled to close to nothing in the two years since Comstock's death. But a new Comstock was coming, like a storm on the horizon. If she did not find a way to escape this house, it would all begin again.

Then she reminded herself that it was only Potts, young, handsome and smiling, and as different from an earl as it was possible to be.

With a snarl, Pepper launched himself from the doorway, making a desperate lunge for his coat sleeve.

He was up and out of the chair in a flash, causing the dog to miss by inches and fall back to the floor with a snap of his jaws.

His action brought a fresh flood of emotion to chase away her fear, as she watched male thighs encased in tight britches uncrossing and swinging clear of the desk, the curve of his hip revealed as he leapt clear and snatched his coat-tails away from the dog. She had to fight the urge to grin stupidly or perhaps to drool, as Pepper had at the sight of her bacon, for her mouth seemed to be hanging open at the sight of him. She closed it and forced her lips into a cool smile. 'Are you afraid of dogs, Potts?'

He returned her smile, probably unaware of the tumult inside her for his eyes never left the dog. 'I normally get along quite well with them.'

'But not this one, apparently.'

He stared down at Pepper with obvious loathing. 'Because there is something wrong with it. Damage to the brain, perhaps. He was rescued from a burlap sack, just as he was to be thrown into the Delaware by a despicable little boy. He came out of the bag, an ungrateful cur who would, quite literally, bite the hand that feeds him.'

Charity produced another morsel of breakfast from a napkin in her pocket and whistled.

The dog sat up on his haunches, wagged and received his treat, taking great care to touch her fingers with nothing more than a grateful swipe of his tongue.

She looked back at Potts. 'I see no such problem.' She looked back to the dog. 'Run along now, Pepper.

The nasty man and I must discuss why he is lounging in the Earl's study, for I see no sign of an inventory in progress.'

'Because I have been busy,' he said, his smile never faltering as he watched the dog trot from the room.

'You have but one job in this house,' she reminded him. 'If not that, what can you be busy with?'

'This,' he said, pulling a folded sheet of parchment from his pocket and handing it to her.

She felt a weird prickling on her skin at the sight of it. Surprise. Excitement. No. It was amazement. She thought she'd known the house well and the secrets contained in it. Her plan had been to tantalise Potts with them, to seduce or control him. But he had produced, seemingly out of thin air, a clue she had never seen before.

The largish rectangle of paper had been folded carefully into fourths and had not a wrinkle in it beyond the creases that had caused. She turned it over, then held it to the light and saw no sign of printing on either side. The only irregularity was a series of small, rectangular holes spaced about the page at random intervals. In some spots the paper was almost intact, in others, perforated so often that it reminded her of lace.

She looked back to Potts. 'Where did you find this?'

He pointed to the puzzle box, which was now resting on the corner of her grandfather's desk and shut up again to be the impervious block of wood that it had been when they'd found it. Without another word, he picked it up and began to solve it, his fingers flying through the steps to reach the inner container. Then he opened that, as well, tapping each side like a conjurer doing a trick.

He set it aside and picked up the case again, completing several more steps until a tray slid out from the bottom of it. Though now empty, it was just deep enough to contain a single sheet of carefully folded paper. *'Voila!'* He gave a little bow and looked at her as though expecting applause.

She resisted the temptation to offer it.

He responded with a slightly hurt expression and offered more information, as if trying to impress her with his cleverness. 'It is a key code of some kind, is it not? The paper should fit over a page in a book or journal and reveal a message. But it is none of the books in this room, for I have checked them all.'

He was right, of course. And the study was one of the places a logical person would search. The wrong one, but a logical choice. It did not explain, however, why he would be reading a diary that was far smaller than the page the key must fit on. That behaviour hinted that, though he was interested in the treasure, he might be searching for something else that she knew nothing about. She filed the fact in her mind and returned to the matter at hand.

'If you are looking for a book, have you considered looking in the library?'

For a moment, his face went blank. Then, his expressionless face split in a dazzling grin. 'There is a library.' From his tone of wonder, she might as well have told him they kept a dragon in the cellar. Surely they had libraries in America.

'I do not know my way around the house or perhaps I'd have stumbled upon it before coming here,' he added. 'Lead me to it.' He paused again. 'Please.'

She smiled to herself, surprised. Had anyone ever expressed an eagerness to see that particular room of the house? If they had, they had certainly not done it twice. Even the family used words like 'gloomy' and 'uncomfortable' when they spoke of it. It was why the space had been abandoned to her. 'It is not surprising that you did not find it, for it is rather out of the common way. Follow me.'

She led him out of the study, making a point to leave the door ajar so it would not disturb her again. Then she took him back past the common rooms, down a hall and then another until they were nearly as far away from the Earl's study as it was possible to be.

Finally, they stood in front of the last door at the end of the furthest wing. Since the key had been safely in her possession since Grandfather's death, she had no worries about keeping this one closed, especially if it preserved her privacy.

Then she opened the door and waited for the reaction that visitors to the manor generally had. He would take one look at the forbidding corner room, shiver in the cold draught, squint into the gloom and ask if it were possible to remove the books they need to somewhere more pleasant.

He stood, frozen on the threshold, amazed.

'This is your library,' he said, undisguised awe in his voice.

'As my family continues to remind me, it is not technically mine. It belongs to the Earl,' she reminded him. 'But previous Comstock heirs seldom availed themselves of this room. Perhaps the estate might not be in chaos if they had.'

'They did not come here?' He stepped into the room, staring up at the packed shelves reaching from floor to ceiling. 'What was wrong with them?'

'The family has always found the room too grim,' she said, then added, 'I am the only one who uses it.'

He gave an indifferent shrug, unable to look away from the shelves. 'A little dark, perhaps. But I would hardly call it grim.' Without thinking, he brought his hand up to caress the nearest leather spine.

He liked books.

It was not such an uncommon thing, really. She understood that a large portion of the population was illiterate. But though some of the people she knew did it grudgingly, all her acquaintances could read.

But she had never seen any of them look at the Comstock library with avarice instead of dismay. Though she did not mind it for research, the room needed light, airing and perhaps a complete redecoration to make it habitable for casual readers. There had been no money for frivolous redecoration in quite some time. Until there was, when the family needed a book they collected it and went elsewhere to read.

But Potts looked as if he had found heaven on earth. Her heart beat faster, as it had on the previous evening, while they'd played chess. The man was almost too perfect. In fact, he was too perfect. At any moment, he would say something disappointingly ordinary. It would break the spell he had cast on her, bringing her back to her senses and saving her from the embarrassment of having to ask for what she really wanted of him.

'The furniture is uncomfortable,' she announced, waiting for him to agree as everyone always did and suggest that they adjourn to the sitting room.

He pulled the book he had been touching off the shelf and dropped into the nearest chair, thumbing through the pages before finding a passage that interested him. 'One could grow used to it, I'm sure,' he said without looking up.

'You are the first to think so.'

He barely seemed to hear, already engrossed in the book on his lap. His fingers spreading on the leather cover like a lover's caress, toying with the cords on the spine, running a nail down the joint. She was unable to contain a shiver of desire and a flush of embarrassment at being jealous of an inanimate object.

'It gets cold in the winter,' she said to disguise her reaction, desperate for proof that he was mortal and disappointing, just like everyone else.

'There is a fireplace,' he replied, then glanced up at her with a frown as if annoyed at her continual insults to the room. Then he set his book aside and rose to pace down the shelves, forgetting her again. 'Where would one even start?'

'To look for the book that matches your key?' she asked, trailing behind him.

He threw his arms wide and turned suddenly to face her, grinning again. 'To read them. There are so many.'

'I recommend, here.' She took his hand and dragged him towards a set of shelves near one of the library tables. 'Perhaps it is not the best method of organisation, but I keep my favourites close. There is Shakespeare, Scott, the poetry of Blake. There are novels, as well,' she said. 'I will admit to the guilty pleasure of reading them. *The Castle of Otranto* is an excellent way to pass a stormy evening.'

'I agree.' He was smiling at her choices, nodding in approval. 'But Thomas Paine?' he said, surprised to find it at the end of the row.

'I told you before that we had books in England,' she reminded him. 'I am sure there are other works by Americans, if that is all you want to read.'

'No. I want…' He did not finish the sentence, but she could guess the rest. He wanted to read it all. He looked back at her, breathless with anticipation. 'My family in America was not exactly opposed to the written word. Though they liked books, there was seldom time or money to enjoy them.'

'You were poor?' she said, surprised.

'Not always,' he allowed. 'Sometimes we had money. Sometimes we did not. A rootless plant cannot be expected to thrive. And a rootless man?' He shrugged again. 'There is no point in accumulating possessions when one does not plan to stay in one place.'

'You will have all the time in the world to read, while you are here,' she coaxed.

He blinked, shocked back to reality. 'I do not plan to stay for ever. And that is how long it would take to enjoy what is collected here. In fact…' He swallowed.

'I do not mean to be here very long at all. The situation here is hopeless. And I have promised…' He stopped speaking aloud. But by the look in his eyes, a conversation that she was not privy to continued in his mind.

Then, as if coming to a decision, he turned his back on the books and looked at her instead. 'I cannot allow myself to become distracted, when there are more pressing matters to deal with. It is time that we are honest with each other, Miss Strickland. I know what you are looking for and wish to help you.'

'You do?' she asked, putting a hand to her breast as another shiver went through her. It did no credit to him if he thought her a frustrated spinster who would be easily seduced. But since it was true, she had no right to complain.

'The necklace you were wearing last night was paste, as is the rest of the set it belongs to. You think the Comstock diamonds exist somewhere in this house and you have been looking for them.'

'The diamonds,' she repeated. For a moment, she had forgotten all about them. It was as if they were playing chess again and she had just lost another piece.

'The Earl suspected they were missing,' he said, voicing her worst fears. 'It is why he asked for an audit.'

Her sister Hope had spent months worrying about what might happen when the Earl arrived and learned that the most precious piece of the entail was missing. But Charity had made much progress in searching for them and assured her that all would be well by the time their American relative arrived at the house.

Now it appeared Comstock had known all along. She had no fears of his being angry, for she knew the stones were somewhere in the house. She could produce them, given a little more time.

But she had not anticipated that a handsome man would arrive out of the blue, smart enough to best her with her own plans but morally conflicted and eager to make a hasty departure afterwards, just as it became inconvenient for him to stay.

'Please, Miss Strickland. Let me help you.' He was smiling at her in a way that was not quite innocent. His eyes held the same glint of avarice she had seen when he had boosted her up the chimney thinking he would split the prize they found.

If he had known about the paste copies, then the only reason he was paying attention to her was in hopes of learning the location of the real stones. It was a good thing she had not actually fallen in love with him, or this revelation would be devastating.

At this, the rational voice in her head offered nothing more than derisive laughter. Apparently, she would not be allowed to lie to herself and claim she felt nothing. The flame of desire at the sight of him had not abated on learning the truth. But it had kindled a second fire of rage that was almost its equal. She had been doing fine with her search until he had arrived and would do just as well without him.

He was the one who needed her.

'You want to help me find the diamonds,' she said, returning the same knowing smile he had offered her. 'And I assume that there is a price for your help, Potts?'

He gave a half-hearted shrug, as if to say talking money with a lady was normally beneath him. But since there was no man about, what else could be done?

There would be a price for her help, as well. She gestured to the chair he'd occupied before.

'Please, sit. Let us discuss.'

Chapter Eight

He had a library.

He also had problems and no time to be distracted from solving them. But it was hard not to be. Shelves around him stretched from floor to ceiling. There was a wheeled ladder attached to them, currently tucked into a corner, but able to run around the perimeter of the room on brass rails, to make it easy to reach to the very top.

And every single one of those shelves was packed with books. Some were in Latin, French and Greek. He did not know any of those languages. But if there were primers, he might learn enough to read.

If he had time.

Which he did not.

He had gone from assuming wealth to assuming poverty. Now that he had seen the house, the truth was somewhere in between. But auctioning the contents of this building would be embarrassing and time-consuming. What he needed was a handful of portable wealth, the sort that could be carried back to America in his vest pocket.

He needed those diamonds. And sitting across from him now was the exceptionally clever Charity Strickland, ready to talk terms.

He sat down and leaned forward with a respectful nod. 'I am at your command, Miss Strickland.'

'First, I must have your word that you do not mean to run off with everything we find,' she said. 'I was not planning to take more than four or five of the smaller stones for myself…'

'You were planning to take them,' he said, surprised. It was odd to be possessive of things he had not even known about a year ago. For some reason, it made him indignant to think of a family member pilfering from the estate. And it was an odd reason indeed, since he wished to do the same thing.

'Only a few,' she reminded him. 'The whole parure has been absent for half a century, I think it only fair that I receive a fee for the finding of them.'

'And what will the Earl say to that?' he asked.

'I have no intention of being here to find out,' she replied.

'You mean to run away from home?'

She laughed. 'You make me sound like a wayward child, Potts. I am a woman, fully grown.'

A vision flashed into his mind of the flesh above her bodice on the previous evening and the calves he had seen before that. 'My apologies, Miss Strickland. But I would have thought, since you are still unmarried, the bosom of your family is still the best place for you.'

'And how long do you suppose it will be so, once the Earl arrives?' she said. 'There is a good chance that

I will be forced into an exceptionally awkward marriage with him, for the sake of the family. I have no illusions about his fidelity, or even his affection. He is like to forget about me the moment the knot is tied. If he does not forget? He will want to mould me into the sort of woman he expects—quiet, co-operative and subservient to him in all things.'

'He is not such a bad fellow as all that,' Miles argued, annoyed that she had formed such an opinion without even meeting him.

'It does not matter if he is good or bad,' she said with a dismissive wave of her hand. 'He is male. In my experience, all men want the same thing.'

'They do?' he said, thinking of the obvious.

'Dominion over women,' she stated. 'Earls are even worse, for they feel it is their right to control everyone on their property. If Comstock does not wish to marry me, then I will be forced into a similarly uncomfortable union with one of his friends.'

'Why would he do that?' Miles said, for it had never occurred to him to do so.

'There will be any number of men eager to curry favour with him, now that he has a title. If he does not know it already, he will soon learn that the family coffers are empty and the land unprofitable. He will find a rich man who is willing to trade that wealth for a family connection and they will work my future out between themselves.'

It was an accurate assessment of the men he'd met in London and their sudden eagerness to help him once they had learned his identity. He had been smart enough to see that such aid came with a price tag that did not always involve money. Some had even mentioned his cousin in Berkshire and her need for a husband. But it had never occurred to him what he might gain in marrying her off to a stranger.

'You think that…the Earl is going to sell you to the highest bidder,' he said, appalled.

'My sisters and I were all destined for such matches, while Grandfather lived,' she replied. 'I overheard him making the plans before Faith had her come out. I was not yet seventeen, but was promised to a baronet of five and fifty.' She snapped her fingers. 'And then he was gone. With no money and no guarantee that an heir could be found, our value on the marriage mart fell precipitously and the suitors did not appear.'

'But your sisters have both married,' he said.

'They have found both love and money,' she said. 'But their first instinct was to find the former, not the latter. When you are told from childhood on that the family exists to preserve the estate, eventually it is almost impossible to separate your wants and needs from whatever Comstock requires of you.'

'But you wish autonomy,' he replied. 'And I suppose there is someone you favour who has nothing of value to offer an earl.'

She gave another short bark of laughter. 'You think I need money for an elopement? You flatter me, Potts. I am a poor relation and a plain one. No man wants me for myself, nor is that likely to change.'

'You are too hard on yourself,' he insisted.

'No harder than society has been, thus far. Before

they found husbands, Faith and Hope refused several suitors for making comments about their "quiz of a sister". It got so bad that I stopped going out with them, lest they reject a gentleman who was perfect in all ways but his assessment of me.'

If this was how she had been treated thus far, her low opinion of men made perfect sense. It made his blood boil to think of the men who had dared to insult her, a woman who had no fault other than a quick mind and an unguarded manner. Then he remembered that it was in his power to right any wrongs that had been done to her and see to it that she had the happiness she deserved.

'Perhaps society has treated you unfairly thus far. But I am sure the new Earl will want to know of your concerns for your future,' Miles insisted. 'If you put it reasonably to him, as you just did to me…'

'You are not an earl, Potts,' she said, with an exasperated sigh. 'You do not have the full weight of generations of nobility, reminding you that it is not your place to accommodate the wishes of others, it is theirs to accommodate yours.'

'True,' he said. At least, he did not feel like an earl. As an American, he found the idea that strangers were obligated to bend and scrape to him disconcerting at best and annoying at worst. He wanted to be long gone from this place before it started to seem normal. 'But suppose that I was. If I had the power to give you anything you wished, what would you ask of me?'

For a moment, her eyes went wide, as though either the question or its answer had shocked her. Then, her control returned. 'You mean to know what I would ask of the Earl. I would not *ask* anything, Potts. I would *tell* him and you that I deserve the right to set up my own household and to keep it should I decide to remain unmarried. If I do decide to wed, I need a dowry that is tempting, but not large enough to attract fortune hunters. And money that is not controlled by the Earl of Comstock, so that I can choose the course of my future without risk of my allowance vanishing the moment I displease him.'

What she sought was perfectly reasonable. Even as little as he had in the bank, he could arrange for her future with the stroke of a pen. Or Comstock could, at least. Augustus Potts could do little but offer her commiserations. 'I respect your right to choose your own future,' he said at last, 'even if I disagree with you on several points concerning the Earl and his plans for you.'

'How kind of you to do so, Potts,' she said, her mouth puckering like a tart cherry. 'But I have no intention of waiting patiently for him to arrive, just so we can see which of us is right,' she said. 'My plan has always been to find the missing diamonds and sell a few of the smaller ones to establish myself. But enough of me. You wish to stake your own future, as well, don't you?'

'That is very true,' he said.

'Then before we go a step further, you must agree to take only a reasonable share. A few missing stones can be excused as loss. But if you think to walk away with too much, I will put my reservations aside and tell the Earl what you have done and he will see you hang for it.'

'Fair enough,' he said, shocked at the vehemence of her threats. 'I will take no more than what you wish for yourself.'

She shook her head in disappointment. 'You surprise me, Potts. I have been poring through journals and diaries for several years and have taken the quest almost to its completion. And yet, after finding one clue, you think you deserve an equal share.'

He had a good mind to tell her that, as the Earl whom she so obviously despised, he deserved as much as he wished to take and she deserved as much as he wished to give her. But that meant that her fears about him had been justified. The money was not even in his hands and he was already thinking of ways to control her with it.

He cleared his throat and made an effort to think as Potts would and be grateful for her generosity. 'You have clearly given the matter some thought. How much do you think is fair?'

Now, for the first time since he had met her, she looked nervous. She rose from the chair and paced towards the bookshelves, then wiped her palms on her skirts as if to hide the fact that nerves had rendered them clammy. Then she turned back to him and blurted, 'I believe you have ways at your disposal that would persuade me to give you as much as you wish to take.'

His first impulse was to laugh and tell her that she must choose her words more carefully, lest he think she was hinting at something she did not understand. But she said nothing more, leaving him to fill in the blanks of her suggestion for himself. And try as he might, he could not find anything else that would fit.

At last he said, 'You cannot possibly be suggesting that I seduce you in exchange for a larger share of the diamonds.'

'I do not think seduction would be necessary,' she said. 'If I am already willing, you will not have to waste time in persuading me.'

He shook his head. 'You cannot begin to know what you are asking.'

'I believe I do,' she replied. 'I want you to lie with me, as a man does with a woman. I believe the Bible calls it fornication.'

'Certainly not,' he snapped and instantly regretted it as he saw the stricken look on her face. Before speaking again, he took care to moderate his tone to kindness. 'That was not meant as a censure of your character or appearance. But, Miss Strickland, you have shocked me to the core. Are you telling me that you have done such a thing before?'

She smiled, as if surprised that he would even consider it. 'Of course not. My knowledge is purely academic.'

'An academic knowledge,' he said amazed. 'Is England so much different than America that they would teach such things in schools?'

She gave him an odd look. 'In my country, they seem to take great pains to teach young ladies as little as possible about all subjects. That is why I am self-educated.' She glanced around her at the shelves surrounding them. 'There are books on the subject, you know.'

'*I* know,' he said, 'because I have spent the last few months in the company of sailors on the passage from America. But how did you learn of such things?'

She walked him to a corner of the library and got down a stack of books that seemed less dusty than the others. Then she set them on the table beside him.

'*Memoirs of a Lady of Pleasure*?' he said, flipping it open to a random page, then slamming it shut again.

'And this.' She held another book out to him.

He glanced at the curling letters across the cover. 'What good is it to you? It appears to be written in Hindi.'

'Sanskrit,' she corrected. 'I learned enough of the language to get the gist of the important bits. The illustrations are self-explanatory.'

Unable to stop himself, he opened it to an elaborate colour plate showing two incredibly acrobatic Indians. He riffled through some more pages, then took a steadying breath. 'If this is what you are using to educate yourself on the subject, I hope you understand that the models exhibit a degree of flexibility not found in most people.'

She snorted. 'Of course. But there are far less intimidating poses in some of the other books.' Her eyes blinked behind her spectacles. 'Would you like to see them?'

'That will not be necessary,' he said hastily, closing the book he held and making a mental note to return to the library and seek out the others when she was not there to observe him. 'So you have no practical knowledge of the thing you are asking of me.'

'That is why I need to ask for your help,' she said, as if her request was simply another leg up to reach a high shelf.

'You are asking me to deflower you.'

'You needn't use such a polite euphemism for it,' she said. 'When I first heard that term, I put a mirror between my legs and was quite disappointed to find that it did not look anything like a flower.'

As if the graphic pictures and frank discussion had not been enough to arouse him, he was now left to imagine Charity Strickland, naked and in curious self-exploration. He took a deep breath to clear his head. 'You do not need to explain that to me. I am familiar with the female anatomy.'

She nodded in approval. 'I hoped you were.'

He felt the beginnings of cold sweat on his brow as his blood rushed south. 'It was not meant to encourage you. What you are asking…' He threw up his hands in frustration. 'It is just not done.'

She arched an eyebrow. 'Really? Then how does the species continue?'

'It is not done outside the sanctity of marriage,' he corrected. 'We are not married, nor are we going to be so.' Especially since she had made it quite clear that she wanted nothing to do with him in his role as Comstock.

'Marriage is not actually a requirement for the act,' she said. 'It is a social convention, having more to do with the man's desire for legitimate children and the transfer of property than it does with what might be pleasant or practical for the women involved.'

'As such, it is a perfectly sensible convention,' he replied. 'Unmarried women are discouraged from engaging in…' he simply could not say the word to a girl he had just met '…in that act, because of the risk of pregnancy.'

She gave him another pitying look. 'There are ways to prevent that, you know.'

He sighed. 'I suppose you have read books on that subject, as well.'

'The library can provide a surprisingly complete education, if one cares to look,' she said.

'Obviously,' he said, then cautioned, 'but some things are not as they are in books.'

'That is another reason I am eager to experience the reality of it,' she said with an earnest expression. 'For academic interest.'

'But why choose me for your partner in this experiment?' he said, still not sure whether to be flattered or appalled.

She stared at him, amazed. 'Why you? Have you never looked in a mirror, Potts? You are quite handsome, you know.'

'I do not give it much thought,' he said.

'That is what pretty people often say,' she said with a sigh.

'Because it is not much of a recommendation,' he said. 'It is a single opinion of exterior appearance.'

'It may be superficial to you,' she said with an angry huff, 'but it is very difficult for me to ignore. When I look at you, I quite forget your willingness to steal your employer's property and abandon your job.'

'Aha!' He pointed at her in accusation. 'You admit that I have obvious flaws. My lack of sound morals should be enough to put you off considering me for…' he gave a wave of his hand '…certain things.'

'Things like marriage, perhaps,' she said, giving him an equally dismissive wave. 'But I am not asking for marriage. I am not even requiring seduction. We can simply have sexual intercourse. Then you may take your portion of the diamonds and return to whatever plans you have made for your life.'

'And abandon you,' he said, shaking his head.

'You speak as if your absence will create a hardship,' she said, confused.

'And you speak as if you will not miss me at all,' he countered. 'You make it sound as if you will lie with me and not give a second thought to it after I am gone.'

'That is not what I am saying at all,' she said. 'Of course I shall miss you, when you go. That is likely to be the case whether we lie together or not. But if we do, I will have sweet memories when I think of you, which will be often.' For a moment, her tone softened in a way that almost made him believe that she had some deeper feeling for him than curiosity.

Then she gritted her teeth in frustration. 'But you are going no matter how I feel or what we do. And I refuse to let you speak of my life as if it will be some great hardship, unbearable without the presence of a man. You are not leaving me in the desert or chaining me to a dungeon wall. Once you are gone, I will be right here, where I have always been, and alone, as I have always been. You will go to where ever you wish to be. Things will be almost as they were before.'

'But you will no longer be a maiden. What are you going to say to your husband, when he finds you experienced on your wedding night?' he said, hoping to frighten her.

'I expect I shall lie,' she said. 'Since you are leaving, soon, our time together is likely to be brief. But I have nineteen years of virginity to draw on. Since whoever I marry is not likely to be as smart as you, it should not be too hard to trick him.'

He wanted to argue against her logic, but she was quite likely right. If she claimed innocence, the gentleman she married would believe her. If he did not, he was no gentleman and she should not be marrying him. Unless shc announced it to the world, whatever they did together would remain secret and harm no one. And though he could argue with her and himself that what she wanted was improper, she was a rational being who had argued the subject in her own head and made up her mind on it before coming to him with her request.

Once they were done, he could move on, just as he had countless times before, from jobs, from women and from anything that had ceased to hold his interest. Then he remembered what lay before him and the fact that, for the first time in his life, he was supposed to be running towards something and not away.

'Are you ready to concede the point, Potts?' Charity said, putting her hands on her hips. The gesture outlined her body under her skirt and made her argument almost more persuasively than her words had done.

'No, Miss Strickland, I am not.' He glanced at her for a moment and said a silent farewell to the body under the muslin before giving her a smile that was polite, firm and distant. 'I regret that I will be unable to seduce you, today or any other day. I am flattered by your request, of course.'

'Of course,' she repeated in a mocking tone. 'But you are unable. I have read about that, as well.'

'Not in that way,' he said sharply and reached into his pocket to produce the miniature of Prudence he carried there, holding it out for her to see.

'Mrs Potts, I presume,' Charity said, in a monotone.

'In a sense,' he said, equally expressionless. 'She is my brother's widow. Her name is Prudence. I have promised to take care of her.'

'And by that, I assume you mean you intend to marry her.'

'Yes,' he said softly.

Charity pulled a handkerchief from her sleeve and removed her spectacles, dabbing each eye once, before busying herself with cleaning the lenses. 'She is very beautiful.' There was a resignation in the words that announced this was exactly the sort of woman she had expected to find him associating with.

'She is,' he agreed. She was also monumentally stupid and more than a little greedy. He would not say that aloud, even with thousands of miles of water between them, but that made it no less true. 'Her looks have nothing to do with my decision,' he added.

'Of course not,' she said, turning towards the door as if she meant to run from him, only to turn back in anger. 'You may claim that physical appearance is superficial and unimportant, Potts. But when men who look like you decide to marry, it is to women like that.'

'I have a responsibility—' he began to say.

She cut him off. 'But when one is not pretty and has a manner that has been described as rude, intrusive and abrasive by all who know them, one learns otherwise. Thus far offers of marriage have been non-existent, as have flirtations and courtship. Even social courtesies from gentlemen have been thin on the ground. At nineteen, I am already a wallflower.'

Her lip trembled, just once. Then her iron, almost masculine control over her emotions returned. 'That is why I mean to take my happiness into my own hands. No one wants me, Potts. It should not be so very hard to believe, since you do not want me, either.'

Someone needed to tell her that there was nothing wrong with her face or her personality that time would not cure. Even now, there was much good about her. If men did not acknowledge that fact, then they were fools and not worth her consideration.

But she did not need words, for she had heard them already and did not believe them. She needed something more. Then, as if it had a will of its own, his hand rose to touch her hair. It was the sort that could not seem to hold a curl, but ran through a man's fingers like silk and lay sleek on the pillow when he took it down at night. It smelled of violets. And her lips...

Her lips were warm and soft as he kissed them, barely parted so that her breath feathered against his cheek before rushing away in a gasp as he wrapped his arm around her waist and gathered her close. Then he touched her tongue with his, gently, and her hands, which had been balled into fists at her side, relaxed and stroked his coat sleeves.

If he had an intention at all when beginning this, he'd have said that it was an act of possibility more than passion. What was the harm in a single kiss if it erased some of the doubts she had about herself? But now that he had started, one did not seem like enough.

He traced her jaw with his teeth before returning to her mouth and entering it more boldly, thrusting more deeply and smoothing her body against his to feel curves that were wasted on a virgin.

Would there be anything so wrong in doing the thing that everyone had urged him towards since the moment he had set foot on shore? He could take her in secret now, as she asked him. Then take her again with the blessings of the church. And she would take his side here, in this house for the rest of his life.

Not his house. It was Comstock's: a man he did not want to be and one that she did not want to marry.

So he broke the kiss and set her away from him as gently as possible. She was staring up at him, the picture of temptation with her hazel eyes wide behind her fogged spectacles, mouth still open as if asking for another kiss. The quickest way to stop this madness before it went any further would be to announce his true identity. She would be rinsing her mouth with spirits and locking her bedroom door before he could finish his apology.

But revealing himself would ruin this moment for both of them. Seeing her like this, with soft lips and eyes full of wonder, he could not manage to do it.

Unfortunately for him, there were more than enough unpleasant truths that he did not need to tell her that one. She was leaning towards him now for another kiss and he put his hand on her shoulder to hold her back. 'That was to assure you that there is nothing about you that prevents me from acceding to your request. If my refusal means you no longer wish to share the diamonds we are searching for, then so be it. I cannot make love to you for reasons that have nothing to do with you and everything to do with me.'

'Then tell me what they are,' she said.

'If you knew me better, you would find that I am a feckless layabout who is not worthy of your attentions. But I am not so bad that I would risk leaving a child here when I must go home to give a name to the one Prudence is carrying.'

'She is pregnant?' Charity said.

He nodded. 'You must see that what you suggested would be quite impossible for me.' But even as he said it, his mind was arguing that the kiss they'd just shared had endless possibilities. 'And now, if you will excuse me, I have business for the Earl.' And, though he hated to admit it, he ran away from a nineteen-year-old girl.

Chapter Nine

He had kissed her.

Before and after, he had said a lot of things, some of which were likely important. But all of it paled beside the fact that he had kissed her. On the mouth. The open mouth. He had done a thing with his tongue that she could not remember reading about in any of the books of the library, which were far more focused on other parts of the anatomy. And, now that he was well-rested and clean-shaven, he had been even more beautiful than yesterday.

When James Leggett had arrived, she had admired him physically, of course. But she had seen that he was instantly drawn to her sister Faith and she had done everything in her power to encourage the bond. The same was true of Mr Drake and Hope. They were both very handsome gentlemen and she liked them as brothers.

But Potts was something else entirely. Talking with him was like she imagined fencing might be. Not the clumsy whacking of swords that she and her sisters used to manage when playing with the weapons that decorated the walls of the manor. Trying to convince him to lie with her had been like the rapier battle she had seen at the end of *Hamlet* when they had gone to Haymarket. Fast but totally in control, each thrust met with parry and riposte.

And then his control had slipped. She touched her lip, feeling the smile forming on a mouth that felt ever so slightly swollen.

It should not have surprised her that he had a beautiful and pregnant fiancée waiting for him in America. Though he claimed to be flawed, she doubted that any of those imperfections was enough to prevent women from flocking to him, nor was he likely to resist temptation when it had been offered by a woman like that.

The thought of the miniature hidden in his pocket made her heart ache at the hopelessness of the task she had set for herself. Did the fair Prudence play chess? she wondered. Did they have anything in common other than beauty, or was he marrying her solely out of concern for her welfare? When he had spoken of his plans for the future he had mentioned responsibility and obligation. But nothing had been said of love. There had been no desire in his eyes when he had looked at the little painting.

For that matter, was levirate marriage allowed in America? Though English men sometimes married their widowed sisters-in-law, it was not legal or approved of by the church.

Charity had a momentary fantasy of charging down

the aisle of some distant church and announcing that there was a just cause that such a union could not be performed. It more than likely proved just how far out of society she had fallen that she imagined making a didactic lecture on marital law. A normal young woman would stop a wedding by announcing her inability to live another moment without her beloved.

It did not matter. All her protests would be moot against the sight of Prudence's swelling belly. If he had got her with child it was right that he should marry her.

If…

Before she could finish her thought, there was a soft knock on the library door.

'Enter,' she called, turning to see the butler standing stiffly on the threshold. 'What is it, Chilson?'

'Will you be taking luncheon in the library as usual, Miss Charity?'

She smiled up at him. 'In the dining room. And supper, as well.'

'Mr Potts has requested that a tray be sent to his room,' the butler said with a nod of approval.

'Has he, now?' He had run away from the kiss and now he meant to hide from her at mealtimes. 'He should not be inconveniencing the staff,' she said, smiling to herself. 'Take him his lunch. But when I see him next, I will inform him that all further meals will be taken in the dining room.'

'He is also welcome at the staff table in the kitchen,' Chilson replied, after a significant pause.

'But he is not staff,' she said, firmly. 'He will eat at the table with the family.'

'But when the family is not in residence—'

'I am the family,' she said, to cut off any further discussion.

Chilson did not sigh in frustration, but she had the feeling that he sorely wished to. 'I will see to it that there are two footmen assigned to the dining room, and another to accompany him, should he need assistance with the audit. And perhaps a maid to sit with you, in the evening.'

For a moment, she could not believe what she was hearing. She had waited fifteen years for the moment when there was not a grandparent or a sister telling her that everything she wanted to do was wrong. Now that she was finally alone and could make her own decisions, the servants had suggestions on how she should behave.

It was all the more annoying that they were right to be worried. But they did not understand that it was Pott's honour that needed protecting.

She gave the butler a firm smile. 'Footmen and maids will not be necessary, Chilson. I do not want or need a chaperon.'

There was another pause that could have contained a sigh, had Chilson been any less disciplined. 'Very good, Miss Charity.'

'You may go,' she said and watched him retreat in silence.

The servants would stop pestering, for the moment, at least. But after lunch, she would have to lure Potts out of his room. That was what the diamonds were good for. Although the kiss he had given her was worth at least one of them, he could not have any until they were found. And to find them, she must pretend to need his help.

It had taken Miles less than a day at Comstock Manor to completely lose sight of his plan. He had come to find something to sell so he might leave the country. Though he'd not been eager to return home empty-handed, he had found nothing in England for him but more trouble. He had most assuredly not wanted to marry some distant cousin, who was a total stranger to him, just because everyone here thought it the expedient thing to do.

One day later, he had been tempted with the prospect of lost diamonds, even one of which might save him from debtors' prison. And he had kissed the very same woman he had been meaning to avoid, as a way to deflect her desire for a full-blown affair.

Worse yet, he had liked it. He was not about to seduce and abandon a virgin, even if she had asked him to do so. But then, he had not thought he was going to kiss her, either. If he meant to do right by Pru, he should not be thinking about doing it again.

There was also the fact that Charity disliked the new Earl of Comstock, on principle. It was a point in her favour, since Miles didn't like being him. Still, should she discover that he and Potts were one in the same, she would not be happy with either of them.

Better to go back to his original plan, find a portable treasure and leave. The best place to find such a thing was in one of the older, closed wings where an absence might never be missed. He took the main stairs at a trot, then chose the middle hall, between the family bedchambers and those reserved for guests.

The corridor was narrower than either of the other wings, and darker, as well, with matched pairs of doors on either side. At the end, there was a change in the plaster of the wall to indicate yet another, older wing. There, the passage widened to reveal more halls spreading out in opposite directions.

He reached into his pocket, retrieved the silver dollar he kept there and flipped it. Heads. Left it was. He walked down the left hall, trying and failing to imagine where he might be in the building as a whole.

The first storey of the house seemed to be in the shape of a large H. But the ground floor was a straight line that widened in the middle like a snake that had eaten an egg. If the lower portion of this wing had not been destroyed, he could not think where he might access it, except from the public rooms of the newest wings.

There was a curved stairway at the end of this hall that might enlighten him, but it was unlit and appeared to end in a brick wall before reaching the ground level. He retraced his steps, pulled a ring from his pocket and began fitting keys into door locks.

The majority of the rooms that he was able to open were sparsely furnished with uncurtained, mattressless bedframes, empty cupboards and rickety benches. But halfway down one side, he opened on the sort of room he was looking for.

It was fully furnished and decorated in a garish combination of red and gold with painted Chinese silk on the walls and heavy velvet curtains on the windows and bed. There were no ornaments on the dresser and no jewellery forgotten in the drawers. The cupboard contained gowns and coats that were at least fifty years out of style and of no use to him unless he meant to waste time picking off the brass buttons and tarnished lace.

But on the other side of the room, there was a rosewood cabinet fitted in brass and inlaid with what appeared to be jade. It was also locked. What could be so valuable that it would be locked inside a chest like this, yet left in a back room and all but forgotten?

There was nothing on his key ring that might open this door. But what was the point of being an earl if one could not take liberties in one's own home? He reached into another pocket, got his penknife and jabbed it into the opening, jiggling the latch.

There was a squeak and the doors popped open. He stared in horrified fascination at the contents of the cabinet. The shelves inside were filled with row upon row of carved ivory ornaments, most no bigger than his fist. The front row was made up of well-rendered animals and fish. But the further back he searched, the more surprising they became. There were fewer animals and more people: couples and sometimes groups of three or more. And they were all as acrobatically flexible as the Indians in the book he had seen earlier.

He closed the cupboard again, wiggling the popped latch until it caught. It was just his luck that the first pawnable items he found were the sorts of things he would be embarrassed to carry around in his pocket.

'Grrr…'

He turned to find his evil, little dog standing in the doorway as if it meant to block his exit.

'Do not growl at me. I saved your life once and have seen to it that you will end it in luxury, fattened on table scraps and sleeping on a lady's pillow.'

The dog plopped into a sit, as if considering.

Since the fight seemed to have gone out of it, Miles walked towards the door so he might leave the room.

At the last minute, the dog jumped to its feet, bared its little fangs and charged.

Miles leapt over it, grabbing the door handle as he passed, closing the door with a slam and trapping the dog inside. He fumbled for the key that would lock it in, then thought the better of it. It had been hard enough to explain to Charity that he would not be making love to her. He did not want to admit that he had sealed her dog in an abandoned room without food or water.

He opened the door cautiously, preparing for another attack. When none came, he called into the room, 'Come out, you miserable beggar. Do not think I have gone soft. I am freeing you for her sake.'

There was no sound from inside.

He opened the door cautiously to reveal…

Nothing.

There was no sign of the dog that had been there only a moment ago. For a moment, he thought of searching for it. But only a moment. It was probably lying in wait behind a curtain or under the bed, ready to bite him when he got close. 'Suit yourself, Pepper.

The door is open. You found your way this far. You can come out when you are hungry, or starve, for all I care.'

He went back into the hall and retraced his steps to the main floor and back to the library. He opened the door slowly and paused on the threshold, as he had above for the dog. But this time he wanted to make sure that Charity Strickland was not currently in residence. After the tumultuous meeting earlier, he was not ready to see her again, certainly not during his current errand.

Once he was sure he was alone, he shut the door and returned to the shelf where she had pulled the books she had described as 'educational'. The word proved accurate for, despite a varied tutelage in the ways of the world, there were things here that he had not seen before.

He had heard of the Cleland book, while in America. Who had not? But he had never actually seen a copy of it. It appeared that the library had both the first edition and several even less reputable copies. There was the Sanskrit manual of love and another book in equally unreadable French, but with a trove of illustrations that left nothing to the imagination. The next books, in Latin and German, were not illustrated. But Charity was clearly fluent in both for she had taken the trouble to bookmark the most interesting pages with neatly written translations. He could not decide which shocked him more, the subject matter, or the scholarly care she had taken in writing words that no innocent girl should know.

It was no real surprise that the rest of the row was made up of art from the Orient, albums of paintings on silk depicting all manner of copulation. After what he had found upstairs, it seemed that one of his predecessors had an obsession with all things Asian. If he had travelled extensively to find such collectables, it likely explained where much of the family money had gone.

But other items might have had been here even longer. The shelf beneath held heavy leather tomes with metal loops set into the bindings showing where they had once been chained to a monastery shelf. On seeing the illuminations, he understood the reason for such security. The monks who had done the work seemed possessed to draw phalluses into even the most innocent pictures.

He closed the books again, taking care to return them to the shelves in the same order he had removed them, to give their curator no indication of his examination. The last thing he needed was for her to realise he had been looking at them again and thinking that he needed inspiration.

But that was hardly the case. While it was certainly titillating, he preferred the actual activity to looking at pictures thereof. He doubted that anywhere in the entail documents, he would find that he was required to preserve and display the extensive Comstock pornography collection for future generations.

But the presence of the things put ideas into his head that had nothing to do with bedding Miss Charity. The problem remained that he had no idea how to carry it out. But that did not mean he did not know a fellow to help him.

When they had met, Gregory Drake had introduced

himself as a solver of problems and seemed to specialise in getting the nobility out of just the sort of jams that he had fallen into. Drake had been willing to take on the daunting project of inventorying Comstock Manor, even after he'd seen the place and known what he was up against.

Then he'd quit the task in the middle and run off to Scotland with Charity's older sister. Miles had found it annoying, but only faintly so. He could not blame Drake so very much. He was beginning to see how persuasive the Strickland sisters could be, when they got bees in their bonnets. But it had been several weeks and the man had not sent any kind of resignation from employment. The honeymoon had gone on long enough. It was time for him to return to work.

Miles quit the library, but could not help looking both ways on exiting, lest Miss Charity was lying in wait to spring on him and demand that they copulate in the hallway. This was the problem with pornography. It gave one ridiculous ideas about what was likely to happen in moments of passion and not nearly enough information about what actually did. Then he climbed the stairs to his room.

Luncheon was waiting there, as he had requested, as was a writing desk well stocked with quills and ink, and paper. It took several pages to outline his requests, but the end effect looked quite impressive on stationery embossed with the Comstock family crest. Then he addressed it to Drake's London address.

He hesitated for a moment before going to the bureau drawer that held his fresh linen and fishing around under a pile of neckcloths to find the signet he had hidden there. Then he took it back to the desk along with the tinder box from the fireplace to melt the sealing wax. He'd vowed, once he'd left London, that he would never use the Comstock seal again. He'd felt like an imposter when signing documents before and was eager to be free of it.

But in this case, it was appropriate. This project was less about what he needed and more about what was necessary to the estate. If the finances could be stabilised, perhaps he could persuade Charity to take on the running of it, even though she had been dead set on escaping the house and having her own life.

But her desire to leave home seemed to have much to do with avoiding the Earl of Comstock. If she learned that the Earl wanted to avoid his responsibilities in just the same way, she might think differently about leaving home.

Now that it was finished, he stared at the properly sealed letter in his hand. If he wished to remain anonymous to the staff here, he could not exactly toss it into the morning's post with the Earl's mark pressed on to the back of it. At last, he tucked it into a coat pocket and made an excuse to the butler about the need to exercise his horse. Then he went down to the stables, mounted and rode to the inn he had passed in the village the day before. Once there, he drank a glass of ale, posted the letter and returned to the house in time for supper.

Chapter Ten

Though she had known him for just over a day, Charity had changed significantly since Potts had come into her life. This evening, when Dill held out a choice of dinner gowns, she chose the more revealing of the two without another thought. Then she sat patiently as her too-straight hair was piled high on her head and secured with pearl-headed pins.

When the maid held out the Comstock necklace to her, she shook her head. Since they both knew it was false, it seemed a pointless addition to the ensemble. Instead, she polished her spectacles and glanced in the mirror. She looked well enough, she supposed. She was still nothing like her sisters, but an effort had been made. Then she gave Pepper a good-luck pat on the head before going down to the dining room.

Potts was already at the table and gave her a sullen expression as he rose to greet her. 'At your service, Miss Strickland.'

She gave him a sour smile in return. 'You have no

reason to be cross with me. Despite our financial difficulties, Comstock Manor has an excellent cook.'

'I could enjoy the food just as well in my room,' he said, staring deliberately down at his plate.

'To avoid me,' she concluded, trying not to sound hurt. 'Do not be ridiculous. Though I made my position plain this morning, it is not as if I mean to spring on you like a wild beast now that you have refused me.'

He started in surprise.

'And in case you have forgotten, we have not yet found the diamonds. Since we parted, the situation has grown much more urgent.'

'In half a day?' he said doubtfully. 'They have been lost for a century or more. What difference will a few hours make?'

'Your employer has been seen in the village. It is only a matter of time before he arrives.'

'Seen, by whom?' he said, glancing around him. 'No one here, surely.'

'He was at the inn, this afternoon. He did not announce himself,' she added. 'But the ostler saw the Comstock stamp on the letter he posted. He told the baker, who told the greengrocer, who informed the kitchen maid who went to place the order for this week's vegetables.'

'Who returned here to tell the cook, who told the housekeeper, who informed you,' he said.

'She told my maid, actually. And then Dill told me. Do not underestimate the speed of local gossip,' she said. 'It is not always accurate, but it is very fast.'

'Apparently,' he agreed with a weak laugh and emptied his glass in a single swallow as if he was no more eager for the arrival of the Earl than she was. 'But can you trust any story that has passed through so many tellers?'

'Even if it is not true, I mean to take it as so and redouble my efforts. I meant to be away from here before he arrived.' Though the prospect of that now seemed as hopeless as seducing Potts. 'But if his appearance is imminent, I suppose I shall have to settle for departing soon after.'

'You have no reason to have formed such an aversion to a man you do not know.' He gave her a sceptical look. 'If it is because you had problems with your grandfather, you will find that they are nothing alike. And though you seem to brood on him, when I spoke to him, Comstock did not mention you at all. He does not give two figs for your behaviour…other than to wish you well with it, of course.'

It was a strangely passionate defence of a man Potts claimed to barely know. But she was having none of it. 'The idea that he does not care about me is almost worse than that he does,' she said. 'Much damage can be done in ignorance, you know.'

'Then when you meet him, you must take the time to tell him what you want.' He tapped his forehead. 'You cannot expect him to read your mind like one of the books in your library.'

'Because speaking my mind worked so well with you,' she said and watched him start again.

'You have made it plain that you do not wish to

marry him,' Potts reminded her. 'What can you have to say that would be more shocking than that?'

'I have ideas on the running of the estate that might not be in line with what he wishes to do.'

His beautiful lips pursed in a thoughtful pout, forcing her to take a cooling sip of wine so that she could concentrate on what he might say with them. 'I suspect he will listen to your opinions, request further information and proceed on them, if he finds them wise.' He gave her a thoughtful look. 'Which he probably will, since he has heard that you are a very intelligent young lady.'

She snorted and took another sip of wine. 'You have not met many earls, have you?'

'Until recently? No, I have not.'

'And you are new to this country, as well. You are still enamoured of the American idea that men can be self-made and rise to great heights based solely on their ability.'

'They can,' he said with an earnest sincerity that made him all the more charming.

She finished her wine and stared morosely at the empty crystal, knowing it was unwise to take more, lest she be seen as intemperate. 'What you believe to be true has nothing to do with the way things actually are. Comstock is Comstock because of who his father was. Or, in this case, his grandfather. He is the last flower at the end of the last branch of the family tree. And I?' Perhaps she had already had too much wine, for she was not sure of how to end the metaphor to account for the fact that women were not part of the tree at all and girls were even less than that. 'Let us simply say that he will not take to my suggestions any better than the last one did.'

'You did not get along with your grandfather?'

'We managed well enough,' she replied. 'He adored me when I was a child. And as I grew he was still quite fond of me. At least he was when I behaved as my sisters did. They obeyed him in all things. In return, he doted on them.'

'And you were not so obedient?' he said.

'He said I read too much and that it affected my mind.' She gave up the struggle to moderate herself and reached for the carafe.

He was on his feet, refilling her glass before her arm was fully extended.

She gave him a nod of thanks. 'Girls are not supposed to think too hard. Women even less so. We are expected to be obedient to our parents and subservient to our husbands.'

He smiled. 'I have already noted that subservience is not your strong suit.'

'It makes no sense to follow a man who is going in the wrong direction,' she said, staring at him. The candlelight made him even more handsome than he was in daylight, softening some features and throwing others into sharper relief. She wanted to stare at him, to drink in every last detail so that she could remember him before he disappeared from her life.

She wanted to. But that would be rude. Instead, she removed her spectacles, pretending to clean them with her napkin and letting her poor eyes render him a pleasant blur.

'And what direction was your grandfather taking that you did not want to follow?'

'The same way his father and grandfather took. The path of least resistance,' she said. 'He sought to preserve the house and the things in it as it has always been. His successor is likely to do the same, since he will be taking the advice of other men who are all doing exactly that.'

'And what would you do, in their stead?'

'If I was the Earl?' She smiled. 'I would get a proper inspection of the house to see if the far wing is even worth saving. It makes no sense to have the rooms if they are falling to ruin and never used.'

'And once that was done?'

'Do the same with the dower house. Grandmama must be provided for. But she should not be expected to live in a house with dry rot and loose bricks. If that house does not suit, perhaps he can rent her rooms in London and designate a suite of the manor for her use when she visits.'

'And then?'

'Then he should sell everything that is not nailed down. What is the point of keeping things that are never seen and never used, just for the sake of posterity?'

'An excellent question,' he agreed.

'And if that is still not enough, he should sell the rest of the diamonds, should we manage to find them. It will be somewhat more difficult to give up such a prominent part of the entail. But we have been managing on paste for so long, I see no reason we should not continue to do so.'

'Those are all excellent suggestions and much in line with what I would have said.' He added an approving nod.

'And there are likely other sources of income that have not been considered,' she added. 'But when I made even the smallest suggestion, Grandfather banished me from the library.'

'He locked you in,' Potts said, horrified.

'He locked me out,' she corrected. 'And out of his study, as well. He denied me admittance to the things I loved and refused to speak to me until I promised to be quiet again.' He had filled her glass again and she drank deeply. 'But I refused to be silent, so the doors stayed locked. That was how things ended between us, for he died later that year.'

'I am very sorry,' he said, in a quiet voice.

She sighed. 'My sisters had no problems with him. But then, they never bothered Comstock with anything more taxing than the colour of the sky and whether it might be wise to take a coat when he rode out.' She stared down at her plate, no longer hungry for the food on it. 'But he taught me that it was better to be alone than to feel alone.' She looked up at Potts. 'The day he died, I stole his keys and unlocked the doors. But I do not mean to stay and see them locked again. I will not be ignored in my own home, or bartered off to marry a stranger, or any of the other things that might happen to me should I stay. I want a say in my own future.'

She was becoming overwrought with the memories, for when he answered her, it was with the calming tone one used on small children and horses. 'I will speak to him. It will be all right.'

'Because you are good at solving other people's problems, aren't you, Potts?' she said, and watched him start in surprise.

'What makes you say that?' He seemed honestly puzzled.

'This afternoon, you said that your dear Prudence was with child,' she said and watched to see if he squirmed.

'Yes,' he said, his face as blank and unreadable as it had been when they'd played chess.

'Not your brother's child, for you mentioned that it was fatherless. But I doubt you'd have left her, had you thought it might be yours.'

'Perhaps you give me too much credit,' he said, admitting nothing.

'I do not think so.' She stared at him, losing herself in his bottomless dark eyes. 'You are not the sort to scatter your seed unheeding of the consequences. If you were, you'd have had no second thoughts on my offer this afternoon.'

'The identity of the child's father does not matter,' he said, filling his own glass again. 'I promised my brother before he died that I would take care of her. I would not be doing so if I let the world call her a whore and her child a bastard.'

'You do not sound very happy about it,' she said.

'My happiness does not factor into the equation.'

He drained his glass, refilled it and drained it again. 'When I make a promise, I do not break it. I told my brother he need not worry and I will tell you the same. You will have nothing to fear from Comstock. You have my word.'

Then he pushed away from the table as if that was all it would take to leave his problems behind. 'But let us speak no more of the future. It will come fast enough without our worrying about it. Let us forget the Earl, the diamonds and everything else. Would you fancy chess? Or perhaps some other game that you stand a better chance of winning?'

He was taunting her. And despite herself, she smiled. 'How are you at billiards?'

'Abominable,' he said, smiling back.

'And you will be even worse on a warped table. This bodes well for me. Come, let me show you the billiard room.'

Chapter Eleven

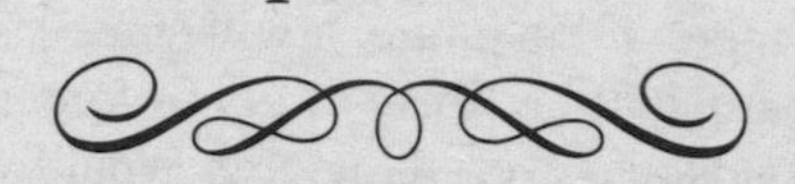

The Comstock billiard room was everything he could have hoped for. Though it must have been empty for some time, there was a faint smell of tobacco still hanging in the air. The walls were hung with trophy mounts and paintings that alternated between hunting scenes and pretty women showing an excessive amount of flesh.

It was a testament to the diligence of the servants that though the house was practically empty, the crystal decanters on the sideboard were kept well stocked with brandy. He poured a glass for himself and, after a moment's thought, a smaller glass for her. They'd both had too much wine at dinner, but to be sober was to remember his duty and his future, and he did not want to do either. He set his glass on the edge of the table and turned to select the straightest of the cues from a rack along a wall.

Charity poked at the fire and surveyed the table. 'There should be an iron around somewhere, so we can get the worst of the wrinkles out of the felt. Try the little Chinese cabinet behind you.'

He turned to the corner she'd indicated and was alarmed to discover a mate to the one that he had seen in the bedroom above. Knowing the sense of humour that gentlemen exhibited when ladies were not present, it was probably not wise to open it in front of her. 'It is locked,' he said, then waited to hear her announce that it never had been before.

'I believe the key is on one of the ledges,' she said, now pointing above his head. 'When we girls wished to play, we usually had Chilson prepare the table for us. But I have dismissed the servants for the evening.'

'I see.' She seemed occupied with choosing her mace, so he turned quickly, snatched the key from its place and bent down to unlock the doors, blocking the sight with his body.

The shelves of this one held an array of erotic *objets d'art* rather like the things he had seen some of the sailors carving from walrus tusks to pass the time on the crossing. 'No iron,' he said, wincing and slamming the cupboard shut again.

'Oh, well. I suppose we shall have to make the best of it, then.' She gave him a wicked smile. 'Shall I set up the game?'

'If you would,' he replied, eager for the distraction.

She removed the balls from a tray on a side table and leaned across the breadth to put them in their proper place.

He took a long sip of his brandy. As she'd sat across from him at dinner, he'd noticed that her gown was pleasantly low-cut. Even lower than on the previous evening, in fact. Without the depressing distraction of a false diamond, he had been able to enjoy the sight of her. But his admiration had been well within the bounds of gentlemanly good taste.

Now, as she bent low over the table, he could see all the way to Delaware. And an excellent view it was. He turned his head, only to find himself staring at a painting of randy cherubs. The opposite way was the Chinese cabinet, which he did not want to think of, much less look at.

As she stood up straight again, he gathered his wits and forced himself to look her in the eyes.

'Now, what shall you give me if I beat you?'

'Eh?'

'Last night, you tricked me into letting you help with the puzzle box. Tonight, I shall name the stakes.'

He took a gulp of brandy, preparing himself.

'I think I should like another kiss, please.'

'No!'

'It is not so much to ask, is it? The one you gave me this morning was very nice and it has not changed anything between us.'

After all he had seen today, he was in a much different mood than he had been this morning. But to tell her so would reveal far more than he wanted her to know about the contents of his mind and, perhaps, his breeches.

'A kiss,' he repeated, to buy time to think. He was quite handy with a cue and she was just a girl who could not be trusted to keep the felt intact without using a mace. He would beat her, just as he had last night. 'I think that can be arranged,' he said at last. 'And if I win, you will stop pestering me about such things.' One game and he would have his peace of mind back, intact, just as it had been before he'd met her.

'Of course,' she agreed. She was staring at him again. 'Well, don't just stand there holding your stick. You may take the first shot.'

He managed to break the balls without scratching, but just barely.

'A terrible shot, Potts,' she said, smiling sweetly at him. 'For you, at least.' She twirled the mace in her hands, holding the tail end of it forward to shoot, unencumbered by the weighted end behind her. Then she leaned forward again. As he was staring at her breasts, there was a snick of the cue meeting the balls. Then, some magic he had never seen before sent them spinning wildly around the table, caroming off banks and each other to end just where she needed them to be.

Over the next few minutes, she avenged herself of every British loss from Bunker Hill to the Battle of New Orleans. Her skill was staggering, her smile sweet and her breasts nonpareil.

Her grandfather's brandy was also exceptionally potent and he'd had too much of it. Why else would he be thinking the things he was thinking about her?

Love.

He smirked at the idea. He had known her for only a day. He admired her intellect, of course. Her good sense, as well. She was a wickedly smart chess player. If she would school him at billiards, he might make his living on it back home. But if he loved anything, he loved her breasts, which were almost falling out on to the table as she sunk the shot that finished him.

Then, she stood up again and her bodice gave a friendly bounce of encouragement. 'Another game? But remember, you will owe me even more kisses, should you lose.'

'What would be the point?' he said with a happy sigh. 'You have mastered me.'

'I seriously doubt that,' she said, placing her mace into the rack and walking around the table towards him. 'Now, if you would be so kind as to give me my reward?' She smiled and held out her arms to him.

And, God help him, he finished the last of his brandy and stopped resisting.

This kiss was different from the last one.

That had been soft and gentle and a little exciting. It had been everything she had hoped for in a first kiss.

She'd had no doubt she would beat him and had known that this kiss would be coming almost as soon as they had started to play. Still, it took her by surprise. It happened a split second sooner than she'd planned, for he had eagerly closed the distance between them as she'd approached. Since he was sure of her consent, he did not bother to hesitate, sealing their lips and taking her open mouth with a sudden, challenging thrust of his tongue. Then he gripped her waist and lifted, balancing her on the edge of the billiard table and stepping between her spread legs.

It seemed that the last few seconds were but a preamble. Now he was kissing her as if she were food and drink and air, as if he could not survive if they were parted. It was glorious. She kissed him back as best she could, matching the movements of his tongue and trying to return the pleasure he was giving her, afraid that at any moment he would stop and she would be alone again.

But when he did stop, it was only to whisper, 'Just one? Or do you want more?'

'More,' she murmured. 'More.'

'You do not know what you are asking,' he whispered into her ear and ran a finger along the top of her bodice, then back up her throat. 'I want to bite you. Here. Here. Here.' His finger tapped the pillow of her breast, the side of her neck and the place where her pulse hammered in her throat. 'I want to suck on your skin like a juicy peach and mark you so the world will know I've done it.'

This was the point where she was supposed to object. But she could imagine his teeth on her throat and every muscle in her body seemed to tighten in eager anticipation. He stared into her eyes and, when he was sure she would not cry off, his hands cupped her breasts and squeezed them possessively, then more slowly, massaging them through the fabric of her gown. 'But anything that happens between us will need to be secret. There are places that I can kiss you that will not show. Would you like that?'

He meant in places that were always covered by clothing. She tried to take a breath to show that she was calm and not the least bit frightened by what she had suggested, but it came out as a wordless gasp. So she looked into his eyes and nodded.

'Before we continue, I must know something.' He touched the tip of her nose with his finger. 'Did you know what was in the cabinet when you brought me here?'

Her reason returned with a thump at the *non sequitur.* 'What?'

He stepped to the side, turned the key and opened the cabinet doors.

She stared in silence at the contents. Grandmama had frequently hinted that her generation was not confined by the current morality and enjoyed themselves without guilt. Charity had to admit that her views towards Potts might have been coloured by the suggestions. But she had not thought that her grandparents were quite so free as this.

Considering that this collection had been locked up tight in a room normally occupied by men, it was possible that Grandmama would be just as shocked as she was to see them. But unless she wanted to risk hearing stories about her grandparents that were even more hair-raising than usual, it would be best not to ask.

She glanced to the man at her side, trying to guess if he wished her to be curious or horrified. At last, she decided to attempt to bluff. 'I have no idea what these are,' she said quickly. 'But if you wish to enter them into the inventory…'

'You have no idea,' he said, giving her a dubious look. 'If you admit to not knowing something, it will be the first time in history. It will also be a lie. I doubt, after the books you have been reading, that there is a gap in your education the size of this.' He picked up one of the smaller pieces and weighed it in his hands.

She was supposed to be shocked. But it was overcome by her curiosity as to the accuracy of the carving, and the size, which still seemed overly large compared to pictures she had seen.

When she did not answer him, he continued. 'Far be it from me to allow you to continue in ignorance, especially after what you have requested from me. The thing I am holding is what the French call a *consolateur*. I have also heard the euphemism, widow's comforter. In New England, the whalers call it a "he's at home". They give them to their wives to keep them from having just the sort of ideas you have been having about me.'

'Really,' she said faintly.

'Indeed,' he said, then glanced at the contents of the cabinet and gestured towards the back row. 'Though the man who carved that one on the left either had a very high opinion of himself or a problem with carving to scale.'

'Of course,' she said, dropping her gaze so as not to be caught staring at the thing. 'That is what I suspected.'

'My question for you would be—have you considered putting such an item to its intended use?'

'You should not...'

'Ask you such a personal question,' he said, finishing her sentence with a knowing smile. 'Proof that I should not take your maidenhead. If I were to ask such a thing, our spirits should be so closely aligned that there is nothing left that we cannot speak of.'

'But we hardly know each other,' she whispered.

'And that is precisely the problem, my pet. You are actively seeking a lover who is a virtual stranger to you and who will leave you soon after. And I do not understand the reason for it.'

He stepped closer, until his lips were barely inches from hers, as if readying for another kiss. 'You deserve a man who will stay with you because he cannot imagine being happy anywhere else but in your arms.'

Perhaps it was true. But she did not want that man. She wanted the one standing before her now. 'But what if no such man exists?' she said. 'Am I to go my entire life without ever knowing physical love?'

'If that is your concern, we must satisfy your curiosity in a way that does not make me—how did you describe it?—scatter my seed unheeding of the consequences.' He gripped the carved ivory in one hand and stroked it with the other before drawing it across her bare shoulder until it settled into the cleft of her bosom. Then he stroked.

She gasped as her nipples tightened at the feel of it, hard, smooth and cool against her skin.

He spoke as he continued to move it, dipping deeper and deeper into her bodice. 'There are advantages for both of us, should you be interested in seeking relief this way. The need for contraceptives, and the fear of their unreliability, would be rendered nil. And when I go, it will lessen my guilt at taking something that should not belong to me.'

'If you mean my body, it is mine to give or deny and not something that belongs to the first man who enters me,' she said, trying to think past the tight feeling in her belly and the wetness spreading between her legs.

'A true statement,' he agreed. 'But men have developed curious ideas on the matter and I find it hard to cast them off just because one woman wants to be reasonable. If I bed you and leave, I will feel guilty.'

'You don't—'

He stopped her argument with a kiss on the mouth. When it ended, she was too breathless to speak.

He had no such problem and continued. 'There is also the very real possibility that I will make a mess of it. I have a history of doing so in other parts of my life. And though I know perfectly well how to satisfy a woman, I have no experience with virgins. There can be only one first time. If yours is horrible, there will be no one to blame for that but me.'

'That could be true of any man I lie with,' she argued. 'Should I wait until marriage and the first time be unpleasant, I doubt my husband will be driven by guilt to a lifetime of abstention. If I decide I do not like it, I will be instructed to make the best of it and that will be that.' She was speaking faster than normal, driven by some strange sense of urgency to arrive at wherever it was he was trying to take her.

'True,' he agreed, sensing her need and speaking slower. 'But that does not make it right. And we are not talking of some hypothetical fellow you have not yet met. We are speaking of me. If you do not enjoy what happens, it would trouble me.'

'If that is how you feel, then I am sorry that I asked it of you.' If he did decide against making love to her, he could at least stop teasing her and leave her alone, before she burst into tears of frustration. 'Forget I suggested it. Do not give it another thought.' She pinched her lips together to keep herself from begging for release and readied herself to jump down from the table.

Before she could escape, he caught her by the hips, pinning her in place, and dragged the phallus down the outside of her thigh. 'Stop thinking of it? Since you asked, I have been able to think of little else. But I have not been able to convince myself that it is a good idea.' She felt hard ivory sliding down her leg and something else, almost as hard, pressing between her legs, where their bodies touched.

'This, however?' He rubbed her ankle, below the hem of her gown. 'Harmless pleasure.'

'I have no intention of using that thing on myself,' she said, trying to squirm away from him.

'I do not expect you to,' he said, leaning forward and kissing the shell of her ear. He let out a breath, slow and hot, blowing down the side of her neck. His teeth brushing the spot he had threatened before.

She gave an involuntary whimper of pleasure as her body readied itself for the sudden release she felt when she touched herself in the privacy of her room, late at night.

He recognised it for what it was and lowered his head to run his tongue over the tops of her breasts as the ivory dipped under her petticoat, dragging her skirts up to her knees.

His fingers were tugging on her bodice, pulling it down. Cool air touched her nipples, followed by hot breath and then the teeth he had promised. 'Magnificent.' The word was murmured against her flesh and followed by a nip and a long, slow draw. Her back arched and her hand cupped the back of his neck, holding his mouth against her.

The sensation was indescribable. Perhaps he was right and they did not need to lie together after all. Surely this was as wonderful as it was possible to feel. Then, the comforter in his hand was pushing her skirts up to her waist. The smooth ivory shaft traced a line up the inside of her leg, pausing when it reached the top of her stocking to rub the naked skin above it.

Her legs twitched to squeeze his hips, ready to close on anything that was between them. He gave her a knowing smile and stepped closer. She could feel his arousal pressing against her, faintly amazed that she had caused it. The world could not be as grim as she thought it if a man like this wanted her, even a little.

He continued to smile, staring into her eyes as the hard thing in his hand continued its progress up her thigh, pushing between her legs, the tip sliding in the wetness pooling there, touching her as she touched herself. She could feel the tension building in her and the nearness of release. He'd had no need to worry about pleasing her. It would be good.

He spoke, in a strange, husky whisper, as if sharing

a secret. 'My only regret will be that I cannot look into your eyes as it happens.'

Her brow furrowed. There was no need for regret. If he waited as he was for just a moment, it would all be over.

Then he dropped to his knees and kissed her.

As his tongue touched the sensitive bud at her core, she felt pressure against the opening to her body, the pain of stretched skin and then the inexorable slide of cold and hard against the soft, hot, wet insides of her.

She screamed.

She could not help herself. After, there was a flash of fear that he might think it was from pain and stop to ask if she was all right. He must not stop, not ever, lest she die of disappointment. Or perhaps it was the pleasure that would kill her, for she was shattering under the onslaught of his kiss and the strokes of unyielding ivory against her quivering flesh.

She panted. She moaned. Her hands tore at her clothing, palms rubbing against her breasts, hips thrusting against his mouth. Was she trying to help, or trying to fight what was happening? She was not sure. But his hand pinned her to hold her still, his teeth grazed her skin and he thrust harder, faster and deeper.

She cried out again as she broke, mind empty of all but him, body conquered, yet triumphant.

His mouth stilled. He withdrew. She felt the stubble of his cheek against the skin of her thigh as he pressed a final kiss, just above her garter.

She stared up at the ceiling, too weak to lift her head, which was heavy and yet so light that it could have been full of sunshine. She could hear him rock back on his heels and the rustle of satin as he pulled her skirts down to cover her legs, stroking her knee though the fabric.

'I must leave you now.'

She sat up so quickly that the room spun around her, as if, in the few minutes they had been together, it had come unhinged from its axis and wobbled loose in the firmament. 'Leave? No!'

'If the servants come in answer to your cry, we must not be found together.' He turned his face from her, as if afraid a single glance might change his mind. 'I will see you at breakfast.' He took a deep breath. 'But right now...I have to go.'

Without another word, he hurried from the room.

Chapter Twelve

The next morning, she was still shaken by what had happened. Potts had been right. Chilson appeared shortly after he had gone, to assure himself that nothing was the matter. She had made some lie about a mouse running across her slipper, which, of course, explained why she was still sitting on the billiards table in shock.

The always discreet Chilson accepted the explanation as gospel. Both of them ignored the fact that she had never screamed at a mouse in her life. If she had seen one, she was far more likely to summon him requesting a small cage, a bit of seed bun and a thimbleful of water. Since his gaze never left her face, she was reasonably sure he had not seen the thing that had actually made her cry out, which had been dropped on the floor when her lover had run away.

Her lover.

Even if she did not say the words, the thought put a giddy grin on her face. She was quite sure she and Potts were lovers now. The lack of conventional coitus was a mere technicality. It was also one that might be rectified with just a bit more encouragement. Potts had proved a most inventive and unselfish partner. It was only polite that she return the favour he had done her.

He wanted her.

This was also unexpected. When she had first asked him to relieve her of her virginity, she had imagined that copulation for men was an instinctive act that would not be refused when offered. His immediate rejection made her suspect that the choice of partner mattered. If he had no taste for her, it was not surprising. She had not expected him to. She had assumed that the act of lying with her would be done out of pity and a masculine desire for release.

But the things he had done last night had been done solely for her pleasure. The thing that Shakespeare had called a dildo was now tucked between the ropes of her mattress and the rest of its fellows were locked away in their cabinet. She was still not sure that she could use such a thing again without embarrassment. But she had done several things that night that she had not thought herself capable of and did not feel the least bit ashamed this morning.

He had not only put her needs ahead of his own, he had taken some time in contemplating how best they could be met and worried about whether he would hurt or disappoint her if he failed. And in doing what he had done in the way he had done it, he had opened the door to what was probably a wide range of activities he would have deemed 'harmless pleasure'.

But he had denied these things for himself to preserve her reputation. He had hurried away to avoid possible repercussions afterwards, even though she suspected that there were things he might have liked for her to do for him. The matter required discussion, education and, hopefully, a great deal of practical experimentation.

When Dill arrived, they chose a pale rose day gown that was positively frivolous. The long white sleeves were caught up with ribbons at multiple points on her arms and the bodice was finished with a sheer chemisette that did little to conceal the bosom he had called magnificent. Pepper accepted his matching bow with a proud lift of his head and a vigorously wagging tail. Then, they went down to the breakfast room to find Potts.

And, as he had on the previous day, he disappointed her. There was nothing but a small pile of crumbs by the place she'd hoped to find him. Today, she took the time to fill her plate and eat before searching for him. The activities of the previous evening had left her with a ravenous appetite. Perhaps it had done the same for him. If he was an early riser, he might have been too hungry to wait for her appearance.

When she had finished and given Pepper a hearty meal of the scraps, they set off in search of him. He had returned to the study again and was sprawled in the chair behind the big desk with her grandfather's recent journals spread in front of him.

And at the sight, her throat closed and her mind went blank. In part, it was for the same reason as yesterday. There was a man sitting in Comstock's chair who in no way belonged there. The man in that chair was not supposed to be young and carefree, nor was he supposed to look up at her and smile in a welcoming way, pushing aside the book he had been reading as if eager to see her.

It was perplexing. She had been prepared to find the new Comstock intimidating because of the power he had acquired. Potts made no bones about the fact that he was a no one come from nothing. But he had put his head between her legs and teased her until she'd screamed. Now, even though she had a hundred questions for him, she could not seem to think of any of them.

'Good morning, Miss Strickland.' His smile was innocuous, his tone polite. It was as if nothing had changed. And yet, everything had changed.

She cleared her throat. 'Good morning, Potts.'

Pepper jumped to the desktop and stood between them, staring at Potts with hackles raised.

He sat up slowly and, without breaking eye contact with the dog, said, 'Your help would be appreciated, Miss Strickland.'

She snapped her fingers. 'Pepper.' She pointed to a divan by the window. 'Sit.'

As quickly as it had come, his protectiveness disappeared and Pepper hopped off the desk and trotted to his place without another thought for Potts.

She tossed him the last of her breakfast. 'Good dog.'

Potts shook his head. 'Amazing.'

She shrugged. 'Hardly so. He is a smart little fellow I am sure, when you get to know him...'

Potts shuddered. 'Hopefully, I will be gone before that is necessary.'

He was leaving. Even though he had spoken of little else since arriving, she had forgotten the fact. She had also forgotten her promise that things would not change after they'd made love. It was time to prove that she had meant what she'd said and get back to business.

She pointed to the journals lying on the desk in front of him. 'I thought I told you that there could be no clues in the recent books.'

He raised his eyebrows in surprise. Then he, too, continued as if nothing had changed. 'There aren't. But on coming here, I was given no restrictions in where I could not go and what I must not see. Since you voiced strong opinions on the folly of the previous Comstock's methods, I was interested in how the estate was being run.'

'And what is your verdict?' she asked, surprised to have been taken seriously over comments that had been fuelled by too much wine.

He dropped the book he had been reading and slammed it shut in front of him. 'His management was disastrous. The estate has been in debt for decades and yet it continues to spend. Each year, the farmers produce less only to see their rents raised. This drives them to poach the deer and rabbits that are eating their failing crops. And those animals are reproducing at a breakneck pace since a family of daughters cannot hunt them fast enough to control their numbers.'

It was an astute assessment for only two days' reading and raised points she had not considered. 'What would you do to bring matters in line again?'

'I would begin by forgiving the poachers for trying to feed their children. It makes no sense to hang or imprison the men who pay the rents. In fact, I would open the land to hunting parties, at least until the deer stop coming directly to the front door and eating the shrubbery. Then, there is the question of the failing crops.'

He leaned forward in his chair, obviously excited by the subject. 'Did you know that foodstuffs grow better when the roots are nourished? The Indians in America had a habit of planting a dead fish with their seeds to make the plants thrive. Perhaps there is some substance we might add that would improve the harvest. At the very least the midden piles and manure should be buried, since it is unhealthy to leave them too near the villages.'

'You seem to have given the matter some thought,' she said, dazzled by the sudden rush of ideas.

'In another life, I might have been a gentleman farmer,' he said with a thoughtful smile. 'I was told my grandfather did quite well planting tobacco. The land was the envy of the county.'

'In Philadelphia?' she said.

He shook his head. 'Maryland. Our house was not so great as this, of course. But from what I was told, it was large and beautiful.'

'You do not know?'

'That was before the revolution. Your army came and burned it to the ground. The money that was left was spent in the cause of patriotism.'

'And I assume your family was rewarded for its loyalty?' she said.

He laughed. 'On the contrary. My father was orphaned and embittered. He had plenty of tales to tell about the time when life was better, but he did little to improve the situation that had been left to him.'

'And what were you doing with yourself?' she asked, remembering that he had called himself a feckless layabout. Perhaps he was, for playing chess for money did not sound like much of a job.

He shrugged. 'Since I had no family money to begin with and could not afford to go to university, there were many paths that were closed to me. But I am not a fool and have made out the best I could. I have written and read things for the illiterate and set type for a printer. I wrote articles for the *Daily Gazette*. I tried my hand at soldiering, but that can hardly be called a job. When my country was invaded by yours, all men took up arms.' He thought for a moment. 'I played a banjo in a tavern. But not well. And travelled about for a bit with my chess set.'

Perhaps he was a wastrel. Though the jobs he had chosen sounded interesting, they were not what she'd expected from a man of such intelligence. 'You aspired no further than that?'

He shrugged. 'I am much better at finding things I do not enjoy than things I do. Thus far, it has not really mattered. I had no wife. No children to support. I have enjoyed my freedom. I always knew that the time would come when I needed to settle. But thus far?' He shuddered. 'I do not like to be tied to one place and am easily bored. When the challenge is gone, so am I.'

'But that must change now that you mean to marry,' she reminded him.

'It had changed even before I left America,' he said. 'When my brother was alive, we pooled what money we had saved and borrowed more, planning to invest in sugar. My brother took our funds and travelled to the Caribbean. But before the plan could come to fruition, my brother was lost to us.'

'Leaving you with the debts and his family to care for,' she completed for him.

He nodded. 'My family is not what you would call lucky.'

'So you came to England to change your fortune,' she said, oddly proud of his plans.

'And found someone who has even more debts than I do,' he added.

'There are other jobs in England,' she reminded him. 'If you wish, I will help you forge what letters and references you might need to appear formally educated.'

'You think I should lie about my past?'

She gave a dismissive wave of her hand. 'When people are so easily deceived, it can be hard not to take advantage of them.'

He gave her an odd look. 'Some day you will be the one who has been fooled. It will be interesting to see if you are still so forgiving.'

'Should it happen, we shall see. But so far, it has not.' She smiled and continued to plan his life to her own advantage.

'And there is still Prudence to consider,' he reminded her.

'You could use the money you are seeking to bring her here, instead of returning to her,' she said. 'Now, with your understanding of the Earl's current difficulties and your progressive ideas, you might make an excellent estate manager. Comstock Manor certainly needs one.'

If his plan was to marry another, he could never truly be hers. But it would be some consolation to have him close by, where they could see each other occasionally to play chess or discuss books. Because at some point in the last twenty-four hours, the idea that he might leave and never return had become unbearable.

'There are several reasons that your plan will not work,' he said in a gentle voice that made her think he knew far more about her feelings than she cared to admit. 'The least of them is the time involved in arranging her passage. She is unmarried and increasing. Even if I could send her a ticket with a snap of my fingers, she is in no condition for a sea voyage.'

'Of course,' Charity said, trying to pretend sympathy for this stranger who had trapped her Potts into marriage.

'And, of course, there will be certain complications involved in raising another man's child.'

'I should not think so,' she said, considering. 'It is not as if you have a great inheritance to consider or are worried about succession.'

'I am discussing my feelings on the matter,' he interrupted. 'The situation will not be an easy one and

I prefer to deal with it at home, rather than starting a new life and a family simultaneously.'

It did not matter that he might do well here, or that she wanted to keep him near. He wanted to return to America. Staying had never been part of his plan. 'Of course,' she said, smiling all the harder and pretending that it had been nothing more than an idle suggestion. 'But if you truly want to go back home, you will need your share of the diamonds. Have you given any thought to how we might find the book we are looking for?'

He was watching her carefully. 'Very little. I was rather distracted yesterday.'

He had not forgotten. He was being so casual this morning that she had begun to wonder if it had been some sort of wild dream. At the very least it must have been far less important to him than it had to her. But now that she was thinking of it, her nervousness had returned and she could hardly look him in the eye. Was she actually blushing? She could not remember ever doing it before, but her cheeks had grown so hot at the vague reference to what had occurred that she was sure they must be bright red.

'I have not thought on the matter of the diamonds,' he repeated, ignoring her flustered reaction. 'But something tells me that you have.' He looked even closer, as if he could read her like the book they searched for. 'I think you know perfectly well where we should be looking and are keeping secrets from me.' He made a coaxing gesture with one of his fingers. 'Do, tell.'

They were fencing again, matching wits for their

own amusement. Instantly, life became easier. She smiled and pinched her lips together, then shook her head. 'Let us see if you can come to the same conclusion without my help. Come with me. We must visit the Blue Earl and see if he can tell you anything.'

Chapter Thirteen

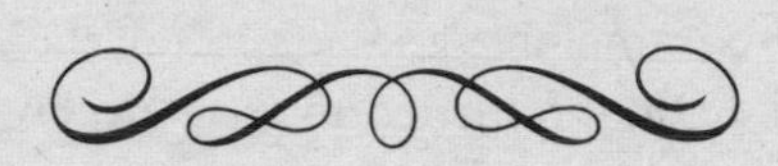

Apparently, they had decided to pretend that nothing had happened between them. It was just as well, since he had no idea what to say to her that would not make parting from her more difficult.

Did you like it?

Of course she had. Women did not normally scream in that way without there being extreme pleasure or extreme pain. Had it been pain, she'd have asked him to stop. Instead, she had thrown back her head and bitten her lip in a way that made her mouth even more kissable.

But while she had been over the moon in ecstasy, the pain he had experienced was excruciating. He should have locked the door, wrapped her legs around his waist and spent himself where she had asked him to be. Instead, he had run, just as he'd run every other time that his life had not gone to plan. He had grabbed a candle from a hall sconce and walked the endless hallways of Comstock Manor until he was too tired to do anything but sleep.

But she looked well-rested and glowing with vitality. The pinched expression she'd worn when he'd met her had disappeared, as had her dowdy gowns and her brisk manner. The gown she was wearing today was quite fetching and bordered on frivolous. She smiled more easily. She blushed. He had obviously done her good.

She had also decided to meddle in his future plans, which were immutable and not part of their bargain. The quicker they returned to treasure hunting, the sooner he could be away. But now she was talking nonsense to him, weighting her words as if there were some hidden meaning in them that any fool should be able to understand. 'The Blue Earl,' he said, then waited patiently for illumination.

'I discovered that the diamonds were missing when I was a child,' she said. 'But I have only been looking for them for the last year or so.'

'You began after your grandfather died,' he said, cutting to the truth before she could tell him.

'It was one of many things he did not want me meddling in,' she replied.

'The missing diamonds were supposed to be a secret between the Earl and his Countess,' he said, then remembered that he could not possibly know something that Comstock had been told by the widow of his predecessor. 'Or so I would assume.'

'Very true,' she said. 'And you were right to begin your search in the study for the book that might hold answers. Until he died, he kept the materials I needed to find the truth in a locked cabinet in this room.' Her smile turned smug. 'Once he was gone, I picked the lock and moved it all to the library.'

'Well done,' he said.

'I have been reading the diaries of the previous Comstocks and believe that the stones were hidden in the tenure of the Blue Earl, during the Wars of the Three Kingdoms. Which means that the book that fits the code key you found must have been in the house at the time of his death in 1648.'

'The Blue Earl?' he said, still confused. 'Would you care to elaborate, for those of us who have arrived late?'

'It is easier if I show you,' she said. 'Come with me to the portrait gallery.' She led him out of the study and to the huge hall that held the family portraits.

'I have not been here since my sister rearranged the portraits,' she admitted. 'The one we will be examining has been gone from the house for several years.'

'Gone where?' he asked.

'To a pawn shop in London,' she admitted. 'Grandmama sold it to pay the butcher's bill. But my sister Hope got it back so the new Comstock will have all his ancestors to greet him, when he arrives.'

'I am sure he will be grateful for that,' Miles replied, feeling guilty again.

'Reserve your opinion until after you have seen the picture,' she said, opening the tall double doors to the gallery. The room they entered was at least forty feet long and lined on either side with full-length portraits of his predecessors, some wearing the ridiculous coronet that had been plopped on his head when he had been dragged to court to meet the Prince.

'Let us work our way backwards, shall we?' She looked up at the newest painting, of a middle-aged man in powdered wig and wide-cuffed coat. He had posed with eyes slightly downcast and seemed to be staring down from the wall in disapproval.

'My grandfather.' Charity gestured to a portrait at the end of the row. 'He did not always look so stern. Unless he was looking at me, of course.' She smiled as if it had not bothered her.

If that had been true, she would not mention it so often.

'There is a painting of my grandmother in the town house in London. But since it is a nude, I have no intention of showing you.'

'Thank you.' He had met the Dowager in Bristol when he'd arrived. Though she was a handsome woman for her age, he had no desire to see so much of her.

There was a glass-topped table beneath the Earl's portrait that contained a row of miniatures. 'My father,' Charity said, stroking a likeness of a man in a clergyman's black coat and high collar. 'That is my mother beside him. And Father's two brothers. All lost.'

'I am sorry,' he said, remembering the diaries he had read in the study and the last Comstock's account of the typhus epidemic that had taken his youngest son and orphaned three little girls.

'It was a long time ago.' She frowned. 'I was barely out of leading strings when we were brought here after my parents died. I remember my uncles. But not them.'

'It must have been very hard for you,' he said.

'I was not alone. I had my sisters,' she said, touching the next little paintings, which were of two stunning young ladies with a passing resemblance to the woman beside him.

'And where is yours?' he asked. If he wished for a remembrance from a lady, he'd have much preferred carrying Charity about in his pocket than Prudence.

'I do not need a portrait to remind me of my appearance,' she said, not looking up. 'I have a mirror.'

'You do not sit for a painting for yourself,' he said. 'You sit for the pleasure of others. Did your grandmother not wish you to do so?'

'I refused,' she said through tightened lips and walked down the row of pictures.

Though she did not like to speak of herself or explain her aversion to being painted, she was a font of family history, able to share anecdotes about each earl as she passed them.

Her words registered with him on a superficial level, names and dates, children and notable achievements. It appeared that the avid collector of erotic art was the brother of her great-grandfather, who had posed for his portrait in odd silk robes and a turban.

Miles stared at the faces in silence, looking for any similarity to himself. His looks must have come from his mother's side of the family for he could find no trace of the Strickland features in his own. If his hope had been to feel a part of this family after seeing it all together, he was not to get his wish.

But he was painfully conscious of the blank wall beside the most recent Comstock. The family had left a place for his portrait there. Some day, if they managed to find an heir to take his place, that man's progeny would be walking strangers down the row, pointing to the Eighth Earl, the one who had taken one look at the job before him and hightailed it back to America.

But what else could he do? If it had been the goal to reclaim his branch of the family tree and keep the Stricklands alive, it had been hopeless from the first. There was no way he could fulfil his promise to Ed and his obligations to an earldom. He was only marrying Pru to acknowledge her child as his. That meant that the next Comstock stood a fifty-fifty chance of being an American stranger with no ties to the family at all.

A man could not serve two masters. Deciding between a brother he'd loved and his recently sworn loyalty to the Crown had been no choice at all.

Without his realising it, they had come to a stop and she was staring at him expectantly. It took a moment to realise that she was awaiting his reaction to the portrait in front of them and not expecting the full confession that was on the tip of his tongue.

He turned and looked up at it.

'My God.'

She was smiling. 'It tends to have that effect on people. I should have warned you.'

'Very true,' he said faintly. The man in the picture looked more like a Shakespearean villain than a member of a noble family. It was difficult to estimate his height against the objects in the background, but he appeared to be shorter than average, a homunculus beside the tall and noble men around him. His wrists were thin where they protruded from his lace cuffs and his calves were bony in the silk hose beneath his breeches. His face was no better, decidedly lopsided so that one eye squinted and the other bulged. His red hair was sparse on his scalp, which was the same pale blue as the rest of his face.

'Cyril Strickland. The Blue Earl.'

'Aptly named,' Miles replied, unable to look away.

'If the family has a black sheep, it was him. Ugly, weak and not long for the world.' She pulled the perforated sheet of paper that they'd found from a pocket in her skirts. 'And, apparently, a duplicitous trickster who wished for his family to suffer in poverty. But that was mostly omitted from the family record.'

He thought for a moment. 'What was included in the aforementioned record? Anything that might give us a hint as to what he meant in leaving that key?'

'Practically nothing was written about him,' Charity said. 'He inherited the title on the death of his older brother. A suspicious death, I might add. Averill Strickland was everything an earl ought to be: brave, handsome and beloved by tenants and servants alike.'

'But not by his brother,' Miles supplied.

'One night, Averill went to bed healthy and woke up dead,' Charity said.

'And Cyril became the Earl of Comstock.'

'But not for long,' she supplied. 'He was a sickly child and grew no stronger in adulthood. He was prone to megrims and fits, and had thinning hair...'

'And the blue skin we see in the painting,' he finished for her.

She nodded. 'He died unmarried, within a year of

taking the title. But I think he used what time he had to hide the family jewels and spite us all. There was much turmoil in the fighting between the Roundheads and the Royalists. If he thought that invasion was imminent, it probably made sense to keep the most valuable possessions hidden.'

'Bastard,' Miles said.

'If he had been, we would not have had to deal with him,' she replied.

'Figuratively speaking,' he added. 'And you know nothing more of him?'

She shook her head. 'There was no immediate family left to write his memorial or to retrieve what he had hidden. They had to hunt far afield to find an heir, just as they have done with the current Comstock.'

She stared thoughtfully at the picture. 'Grandmama claimed to be impressed with the American. But she said he had been ill.'

'Seasick,' Miles said hurriedly. 'It was a difficult crossing.'

She glanced sharply at him. 'I thought you arrived separately.'

'We travelled the same ocean,' he insisted. 'There is nothing delicate about Comstock's constitution, if that is what you were implying.'

She gave him another searching look and he regretted making such a strident defence of a man who he'd claimed he barely knew. 'Even if he is the picture of health, it makes no sense to haul him from the other side of the globe and drop him into a seat in Parliament,' she said. 'If there is no one nearer, then perhaps it is time to admit that the Stricklands have had a good run but are ended.' Then, she smiled at him. 'Of course, you would not have come here, had they done that.'

'Very true,' he said. Truer than she knew. A few days ago, he would have told her how heartily he had wished he'd never heard of the Earl of Comstock. Now? He was not quite so sure.

To distract her, he pointed at the painting. 'Where is he standing, do you think?' In the shadowy background of the painting, they could see what appeared to be stone walls and some sort of statue, perhaps a saint or an angel, and a greenish tinge to the light, as though it were filtered through coloured glass. 'Could it be a church?'

'None I am familiar with,' she said. 'It does not look like the one in the village.'

'It was a bit late for repentance, if he committed fratricide,' he replied, then stared at the picture's background. 'Help me take it down.'

One on each side, they reached up and lifted the portrait down from its hook, then struggled it to the floor. Then he reached into his pocket for a handkerchief and spat into it.

'What are you doing?' she asked, startled.

'Some necessary cleaning,' he said, dabbing at the paint with the dampened cloth. 'It will do no harm. But there is something I must see.'

'I don't suppose you can make it worse,' she said and pulled a smaller, lace-trimmed hanky from her own pocket, spat in a most unladylike way and offered it to him.

Between the two linens, he managed to remove the grime from the area of the canvas that most interested him. Behind the murderous Earl there appeared to be a raised dais and a long marble altar. In the centre sat a large book, lying open on a metal stand. 'Do the Stricklands have a family Bible?'

'In the parlour,' she said.

'I think it is time that we pay it a visit,' he said.

Chapter Fourteen

She had been right about him.

Although he did not have her depth of knowledge about the family's past, it had had taken only one nudge from her and he had found his way to the next step in the puzzle. Nor had she known that it was possible to clean an oil painting by expectorating on it. Or that it was a good thing to nourish plants with dead fish.

The depth of his understanding was awe-inspiring.

Now he stood before the family Bible, staring down at the handwritten record of births and deaths at the front, as if searching for some key there. His finger traced names, pausing now and again as if they held some meaning for him and were not just an extension of the history lesson she had given him in the portrait gallery. Then he began flipping pages, as if suddenly remembering his reason for being here. 'May I see the key, please?' He held out his hand for the paper and she retrieved it from her pocket.

He set it against a single page and looked through

the windows. 'Not the printed text, then. The spacing is all wrong.'

Then he flipped to the back and the empty signature that had been sewn in after The Revelation. He glanced up at her. 'Sermons?'

She shrugged. 'More than one earl has fancied himself as a bearer of the Lord's truth. Having read some of their work, I have my doubts. But there is one in particular that will interest you.'

He read through some of the pages, making occasional faces of disgust or disbelief. Then he came to the one she had thought of. 'Averill Strickland?'

'The Blue Earl's brother,' she confirmed.

'Have you already read it?'

She shook her head. 'I decided it might be nicer to do it together.' The thought surprised her. Her sisters often chided her for her need to be right, to be first, to be the cleverest one in the room. But with Potts, it had not seemed so important.

He glanced at the writing desk, then said, 'I doubt we will need to write the message down, for we are both likely to remember it verbatim.'

She nodded, surprised again at how ready he was to put confidence in her and how easily they understood each other. Then, very deliberately, she remembered the face of the woman in the picture that was resting in the breast pocket of his coat. It did not matter that they were perfectly suited. He was a man of honour and had promised himself to another. For his sake, she hoped that Prudence was as smart as she was beautiful and worthy of his loyalty.

He had fitted the paper key over the handwritten sermon and began to read. 'To the right and noble man who finds my message.' He paused to glance at her with a smile. 'Let greed not be your guide in looking for what is left of the things right and fully left to you. Seek ye first the kingdom of God.' He looked up again, waiting for her opinion.

'That is all?'

'There are some windows that do not align,' he said.

'Turn it over and read again.'

He flipped the page. 'Three. For. Too. One.'

She glanced over his shoulder. 'They are meant to be numbers.'

'So it would appear.' He turned the key over again. 'And on this side, we have right, left, right and left, hidden amongst the text.'

'It is a pattern of some sort,' she said. 'Doors or windows.'

'Rooms,' he suggested.

'Bricks in a wall.'

'Stairs,' he added. 'There are so many possibilities that it will be difficult to choose one without some sort of starting place.

They both sat, thinking in silence.

'How much of the house existed, while he was alive?' he asked.

'None of the parts we are inhabiting,' she replied.

'So whatever this pertains to would be happening in an older, unfamiliar part of the house,' he concluded. 'And you did not recognise the statue that was in the background of the portrait.'

'It is nothing I have seen here,' she said. 'And my sisters and I explored every room we had access to.'

'Were any of them fitted out as a chapel? Because Cyril has suggested that we seek first the Kingdom of God. I can think of nothing else that would fit the bill.'

She had been hoping that he would arrive at any other conclusion than that one. But it was the logical answer. 'There was a chapel in the oldest part of the house. It would have still have existed when Cyril was alive.'

He frowned at her. 'That does not sound very encouraging.'

'Come with me and I will show you the next problem we face.' She led him out of the parlour, up the main stairs and back into the central wing. At the end of it she paused to get her bearings, then turned right. And then, to the end of the hall and down what had been a main staircase, some time long before she was born.

Potts trailed behind her, gaping in amazement at the high ceilings and many doors. 'Did the family need all this space?'

'My family gives little thought to what it needs,' she said. 'There used to be many of us. Enough to occupy a castle. Then a manor would have sufficed. Then a large house would have been enough. Now we could manage with a few rooms in London.'

She had led him down the stairs and through a ballroom that might have been useful if they'd had enough money for lavish entertainments. Now it stood as a sad and empty testament to a once-great family.

She escorted him to the end of the room, beneath the musicians' gallery, to a stone wall that did not match the other three, and a Gothic archway. 'The Stricklands no longer need so much space. But we never throw anything away. Not a button, not a book, not a room.'

She put her hand on the stones that filled the arch, which were just as dark and heavy as the rest of the wall. 'We do, however, occasionally brick them up.'

'This is the chapel?' he said, pressing his hands against the wall as if he expected it to move.

'I believe so. I have no proof, of course. But that is what we always imagined it must be.'

'You closed it off.'

'My ancestor,' she reminded him.

'Of course,' he agreed.

'As a country, England has sometimes disagreed as to whether we should be Catholic or Protestant. One of the Earls of Comstock decided it was best that we be neither.'

'How refreshingly humanist,' he said, slapping his palm against the wall in frustration. 'Shall I find a hammer and get to work?' He slipped out of his coat and prepared to roll up his sleeves.

She opened her mouth to object, then closed it again, overcome with a sudden desire to see his arms bared and taking physical action. Then she shook her head both to clear it and to indicate the negative. 'Let us not be so drastic until we are sure of what we are doing. I am not even positive that this was the chapel. For all we know, knocking a hole here will lead us directly out into the garden.'

He gave her a sheepish smile and slipped back into his coat. 'Or into another room that was built over the remnants of what had been here. Forgive my impetuous nature. We Americans pride ourselves on being men of action. But I must not carry the behaviour to excess.'

A man of action with the heart of a scholar and the instincts of a chess player. She swallowed, thinking of the easy way he had lifted her up into the chimney and on to the billiard table the night before. He was staring at the wall, giving her an excellent view of his flawless profile and running his long, deft fingers over the seams in the joinery. Now he turned to pace off the length of the room, frowning as he calculated the dimensions in his head.

If he'd thought that he had escaped by giving her the tools to her own pleasure last night, he had been utterly wrong. Though she knew it was unwise, she still wanted him every bit as much as she had before.

He looked back at her now, totally unaware of the thoughts that were foremost in her mind. 'Are there architectural plans for the house and its additions? I doubt such grand work could be done without them. And for the life of me, I cannot manage to envision how the parts of this house that I have seen of it can connect to make the whole.'

'It is very confusing,' she agreed. 'If plans exist, they are likely to be in the library with everything else of value.'

'Let us go and look,' he said, glaring a challenge at the sealed doorway. 'I refuse to give up when we are so close.'

* * *

As they retraced their steps back through the baffling labyrinth that he'd inherited, Miles tried not to look at the swaying hips of the woman in front of him. She had still made no mention of what had happened in the billiard room. But he, at least, was thinking of it more and more, as time passed.

The search for the diamonds should be paramount in his mind. His trip into the village yesterday had aroused far more curiosity than expected. It was only a matter of time before someone described the Earl to one of the servants and the whole house realised who he was. If they could manage to find the stones today, he might be gone by morning without being forced to reveal any difficult truths.

And that would give him one last night with Charity Strickland. Like the search for the missing jewels, he had uncovered far too much of her to walk away unsuccessful. If the point of last night's experiment had been to bring matters to a satisfactory conclusion, it had failed. Judging by her screams, she had been satisfied. He had not. His desire for her had not been blunted by sleeplessness or exercise, though a few hours spent reading the accounts of the Comstock finances had done much to depress his spirits.

Of course, it had also given him ideas. With a progressive peer in control of the land, it might be possible to turn the tide of failure and salvage some of what had been built. Though he could not stay to do it himself, it might take some time for his replacement to be found. Until then, he might give Charity the power to implement her own ideas in his absence. At the very least, he could write her a formal letter from Comstock, assuring her that she had nothing to fear from him. Her future would not be some bargaining chip to refund the estate.

They had come back to the front of the house and she was talking to the butler and ordering that tea and sandwiches be brought to the library so that they could continue their research. They would be alone together in a room full of erotica, at the far end of the house in a location that was more remote than the rather risky choice the billiard room had been.

Disaster was inevitable. And yet he could not manage to be bothered by it. They would be together all afternoon, either in the library, or investigating corners of the house that no one visited without a reason. What happened would happen and he would deal with the consequences afterwards. Whatever it was that he felt for her, it was futile to resist. He would follow her to his own damnation, if that was what she wanted. For today, at least. Tomorrow, he might be gone.

She had completed her orders and started down the hall to the library. But before he could follow her, Chilson stepped into his way. 'A moment, Mr Potts?' The butler managed to phrase the words in a way that was both a question and a demand.

'Of course,' he said, smiling at the servant as Charity went on towards the library, oblivious.

'Last evening, there was a commotion that disturbed the staff. It sounded rather like a woman's scream.'

'Perhaps it was after I retired,' Miles said, trying to look innocent.

'When I went to investigate, Miss Charity informed me of a difficulty in the billiard room,' Chilson said, his face expressionless. 'She had been startled by a rodent.'

'How surprising,' Miles responded. 'Are rodents often a problem at Comstock Manor?'

'We have mice, occasionally,' the butler admitted. 'But she is not normally bothered by them. Therefore, I suspect it was a rat.'

'Really,' Miles said.

'A rather large one, I should think. One that has recently found its way into the house and is unaware of how hard the staff work to keep the family safe from vermin.' There was a slight constriction of distaste around his mouth as he looked at Miles. It did not bode well.

'That is most commendable of you,' Miles said, feeling much less confident than he had before.

'The footmen have been equipped with large hammers. I have informed them that, should the rat alarm her again, they are to hit it with all their might and evict it from the house,' he said, with a final nod.

'An excellent idea,' Miles said, trying not to imagine the feel of a hammer blow, delivered without warning. Then he added, 'We all want what is best for Miss Strickland, I am sure.'

'It gratifies me to hear it, Mr Potts,' Chilson said with a smile, stepping aside to let him pass. 'Please inform Miss Strickland that the tea tray will be there directly.'

'Thank you, Chilson.' Then Miles turned his back on the servant. After waiting a moment to see if he was struck down where he stood, he walked down the hall to the library.

Chapter Fifteen

'More tea, Potts?' Charity smiled as she filled his cup, trying to catch his eye.

'Thank you,' Potts said without looking up. He had spread the plans she had found for him out on the library table and was trying to fit them together, one on top of each other like overlapping pieces of a puzzle. 'I thought I was clever, but I can make little sense of this.'

She put down the teapot and picked up a pencil. 'We are here. Here are the main stairs.' She found another page and slid it part way under the first. 'This is the old house and fits here.' She pulled it out again and crossed out several of the rooms. 'So these have been torn down, replaced or repurposed.'

She looked up to see if he agreed with her assessment and found his attention remained resolutely on the papers in front of them.

Had something happened in the last few hours? She would not have described him as overly familiar, over the course of the morning, but there had been an easy camaraderie between them that was lacking now. Since coming to the library, his manners had been perfect and his behaviour unexceptional.

Too perfect. Too unexceptional.

She had not expected to be swept from her feet the moment the door had closed. But she had hoped that there might at least be a smile to prove that he still enjoyed her company.

She reached across the table for another plan, brushing her arm against his coat sleeve. As she did so, she was sure she felt him flinch.

She dropped the paper on top of the others. 'This is the second floor. Where the bedrooms are.' She made a large X over the Tudor Room. 'You are here.' Then, she tapped the pencil repeatedly on the paper and stared at him. 'This is my room.'

He looked up slowly, his eyes smouldering. 'I realise that.'

'And what do you mean to do with this knowledge?' she asked.

'Absolutely nothing,' he said, looking away from her again.

'After last night?'

'Last night, we were careless,' he said, through gritted teeth. 'The servants are aware of what is happening between us.'

'And they know better than to question me on it,' she said.

'So they questioned me, instead,' he replied.

'Are you afraid of them? If so, I will tell them to leave you alone.'

By the fierce look he gave her, she knew that she had spoken wrong. 'I am not afraid of the servants. I am in agreement with them. You deserve better than a man who has nothing to offer you and does not mean to stay longer than one more night.'

'One night?' Did he really mean to leave so soon? 'Are you not even going to attempt an audit?'

'I see no point in it,' he said. 'Even if I could account for every silver spoon and stick of furniture, it would take months to arrange for the sale of them. I do not have that kind of time.'

'Prudence,' she said, hating the word.

'I wrote to her as soon as I received her letter and promised her that it would not be long until I returned.' He shook his head. 'She was fine when I left. But that was nearly four months ago. She is running out of time. And since we cannot find the diamonds...'

There was no reason for him to stay. They both knew it was true, but she did not want to hear him say so. 'There might still be hope. There are a few journals I have not read.'

'We know where they are. But short of tearing down a wall of the ballroom, I don't know what good the knowledge will do us,' he said. 'I will write to Comstock and make certain recommendations that will provide for your future. But as for mine?' He gave her a sad smile. 'It would be best if I fill my valise with the second-best silver and be on my way.'

'You cannot...' But she had no idea how to end the sentence. She could not tell him that she would die without him. She had never believed in such melodramatic displays. She had promised that she would let him go without argument when the time came. She had been sure that she had no heart to break.

'We are not finished,' she said, at last. 'We have not...'

He touched a finger to her lips to stop her from speaking. 'I am afraid we are,' he said. 'I am ashamed that I had to be reminded of the fact by Chilson. But what I said yesterday evening is still true. I cannot do more than I have done already because I am not the sort of man who would lie down with a virgin who has only the most superficial interest in me, to satisfy her curiosity and my personal desires.'

'But you want to,' she said, remembering how he had been in the billiard room. 'And so do I.'

'And we both know that it is dangerous in more ways than one to be governed by fleeting desires,' he said. 'We have but to look at the trouble caused by Prudence and a long string of Comstocks to see that.' Then, he leaned forward and kissed her, quickly and with lips firmly closed so she would not take the wrong meaning from it. 'And now, if you will excuse me? I need to find myself a sideboard to pillage.'

Charity sat silent, as Dill combed out her hair and prepared her for bed, ignoring the maid's attempts to chat. If she had not managed to speak today, when the words might have made a difference to Potts, she did not want to begin talking now that he had gone to his room. After he had left, she had pored over house plans and journals for the better part of the day, not bothering to change for dinner and asking for a tray to be brought to the library. Chilson was probably disappointed to find that there was no need at all for a chaperon. The man he'd feared had decided she was not worth the effort.

She had hoped to find some scrap of information that might change his mind and convince him to search a little longer, but in the end, it had come to naught. The house as she remembered it had little to do with what it had been when any of the parts had been built. The combined plans showed a tangle of rooms that had been demolished and built over, or repurposed, or sealed. Doorways and stairs had been added or removed on the whim of the current occupants. Very few of them had kept proper records of what they'd done and when they'd done it.

At any time in those long disappointing hours, she could have given up and found him so that she might tell him the truth. What had started as physical desire on her part was growing into something far more complicated. It did not matter that what she felt for him could have no future. The thought of him disappearing from her life tomorrow was almost too much to bear.

If she had given him some indication of a deeper attraction than physical desire, then he might have been more receptive to her overtures. Instead, she had let him continue to think that what she wanted was nothing more than lust. He had rejected her not because he did not like or want her. He had rejected her because he thought she was as shallow and easily seduced as the woman he meant to marry.

Now Dill had left her and Pepper was sound asleep on the end of her bed, unaware that she had not joined him. The house was quiet. But Charity felt as if she would never sleep again, unless the gulf she had created between herself and Potts had been breached. It might not change the way he felt about her, but she doubted it would make things any worse.

She rose from the dressing table and left her room, creeping nightgowned and barefooted down the length of the family wing and then down the even longer guest wing, until she arrived at the door of the Tudor Room.

Then she paused, realising how foolish and impulsive her plan was. She could see no light coming from the crack under the door. He might already be asleep. Even if he was awake, he might feign sleep and refuse to answer the door when she knocked. Since he had not even bothered to wish her goodnight, she had no reason to think he would welcome her company, once the lights were out.

But if he was taken unawares, he could not refuse her. She had but to open the door. If he was asleep, she would sneak away again. And if not?

She knocked once, then opened before her nerve failed her.

Though the room was lit only by moonlight and the banked fire, he was not asleep. He stood at the window, his back towards her, staring out into the garden. And he was naked. She had wanted to tell him that it was not just his appearance that she admired. But good Lord above, he looked like Michelangelo's *David* must look from the rear.

But much angrier. For when he turned to see who had interrupted his privacy, his face turned from pensive to irate. 'Miss Strickland, avert your eyes!'

She did as she was ordered, but not before she caught a glimpse of him grabbing for the shirt that hung on the back of a chair and throwing it over his head. Then he was stalking across the room, hand already outstretched to grab her and put her out.

She dodged to the side before he could reach her, closing the door as she did so. 'Please. Wait. I need to talk to you.'

'Whatever it is can wait until morning,' he snapped, reaching for the door handle.

She moved in front of him, pressing her shoulders into the closed door and hiding the handle behind her body. 'What point is there in waiting? You are an early riser and I will no doubt wake to find that you have already gone.'

By the stricken look he gave her, it was clear that she had guessed the truth.

'Before you go, I must speak. I was not totally honest with you. And I cannot let another minute pass without correcting the mistake I have made.'

Now that the moment had come, she was afraid to meet his gaze, lest it show that her feelings were not reciprocated. But it did not help to look down, either. That only made her aware of the bare feet and legs beneath his shirt and the curious way the front of the hem seemed to jut out, away from his body.

'Speak, then.' The words came in a low growl, as if he was more animal than gentleman.

'This afternoon, you seemed to think that my reasons for wanting you as I do were trivial. You seemed to think that it was nothing more than your good looks that attracted me. You thought my desire was some passing fancy and I did nothing to correct you. But that is not the truth.'

'Then what is?' he snapped. 'Are you attracted to my fortune? My good name?'

'You are the most brilliant man I have ever met.'

When he did not respond, she gathered her courage and looked up. He was frowning, but from confusion rather than anger.

'The way you outsmarted me at the dower house. The way you beat me at chess. The puzzle box. Everything,' she said, holding her hands out to him in a gesture of defeat. 'I have never met anyone who could do those things. And when you did…' She dropped her hands to her side. 'I do not know how to talk to men. And your looking the way you do should make it impossible to speak to you at all. But somehow, when I am with you, everything seems easier.'

'Everything?' he said and she saw the beginning of a smile.

'Almost everything,' she corrected, suddenly very conscious of the lateness of the hour and the thinness of her nightclothes.

'I wish I could say the same of you,' he said with a sigh. 'You have the quickest mind that I have encountered, male or female, though you are only a slip of a girl. And you are excellent company.' He took a step closer. 'But when I am with you, nothing is easy. I cannot seem to think straight and my common sense all but disappears.'

'Is that bad?' she whispered.

'We will decide tomorrow, when I have to leave,' he whispered back. 'But I would like to spend tonight with you.' Then he leaned forward and kissed her. His lips moved to her cheeks, her eyes and her hair, before returning to her mouth, settling there, coming home.

It was even better than it had been in the billiard room, for there were not so many troublesome clothes in the way as he held her. His bare legs were touching hers, the hairs on them tickling her. She could feel each muscle in the arms that held her. And it took only a tug of his fingers to open her nightgown and push it down her shoulders. She gasped as the cloth slid away, leaving her breasts uncovered.

At any moment, he would explain why what she wanted more than anything in the world could not possibly happen. Then he would send her back to her room. She had prepared an argument to counter his rejection, but it did not come. Instead, he was staring down at her breasts in silence. Then his hand reached to touch them, a featherlight brush of his fingers that made her gasp. He smiled at her response and covered one of them, then nodded with satisfaction at the way it seemed to fit perfectly in the palm of his hand.

He was not stopping. Perhaps it was her imagination, but when she stared down, the prominence beneath his shirt seemed to be increasing. And he did not seem to mind her curiosity, nor order her to look away as he had a few moments ago. She forced herself to look up, into his eyes. 'Does this mean…?'

Potts was smiling at her now. 'Having second thoughts? It is not too late to turn coward, you know.'

No,' she said hurriedly. 'But thus far, you have been adamant that we must not do what I think we are about to.'

He sighed. 'That was before you flattered my intelligence. You are the first woman to do so and I find it difficult to resist.'

'Only difficult?' she said in a voice made breathless by his touch.

His hand rubbed her nipple as he shrugged. 'There is also the fact that you have surprised me at bedtime and we have very little clothing between us.' He kissed the side of her throat before continuing. 'It has left me fully aroused and incapable of begging you to think of your future.'

'And after last night, there is probably not much of my innocence left to preserve.'

'You would be surprised,' he said. Then his mouth took her breast and she decided she had been wrong. He drew her nipple into his mouth and as he suckled, one of his hands lifted her skirt and touched her, entered her and thrust in time with his pulls. The climax that resulted was sudden and short, and she had to cling to his shoulders to keep from collapsing to the floor.

He raised his head and kissed her mouth again. 'No scream tonight? I must try harder.'

'You have not yet given me what I asked for,' she said, trying to be glib.

'And what is that?' he said. His finger moved inside her again.

'More,' she said, at last, still unable to say the necessary words, though she knew them well enough.

He took her hand from his shoulder and dragged it down his body, wrapping it around his erect manhood through the linen of his shirt.

She nodded. 'Inside me.' Then she released him and reached under his shirt to hold him properly.

He sucked a breath in through his teeth and released her to yank the shirt over his head and throw it to the floor. Then he put a hand over hers, guiding her exploration. She stroked, amazed. He was not as hard as the thing that he had used on her in the billiard room. But he was warm and alive, large and still growing in her hand as she touched him.

She had said that how he looked did not matter. But that was not totally true. 'May I look at you?' she whispered.

'If you return the favour,' he said. He moved out of her grasp and pulled her nightgown over her head, leaving her as naked as he was. Then he took her by the hand and led her to his bed, opening the curtains so the moonlight might stream in and touch their skin. He climbed in, lying on his side and patting the mattress beside him.

He was looking at her. For a moment, she forgot to indulge her own curiosity. He opened his mouth to speak and she put a finger to his lips to stop the words. If he said them, she might not believe. But the look in his eyes right now said that, for tonight at least, she was beautiful and he loved her.

Only then did she allow herself to enjoy him, with her eyes and her hands. His hard, flat nipples were almost hidden in the cloud of dark hair on his chest and a line of it trailed down his stomach to the place she had touched him. Now she traced it with her fingers, wrapping one hand around him, cupping the sack beneath with the other.

He gasped again.

'I am not hurting you?' she asked, prepared to withdraw.

'Please, continue,' he said through clenched teeth. 'I will tell you if it becomes too much.'

'Too much,' she repeated, trying to imagine what it would be like to push him beyond his limits.

'If you continue touching me, I will lose control.' He took a shaky breath as her hands moved on him. 'But it might be for the best. I should not spend inside you.'

'Because of the risk of making a child,' she said. She felt a bead of moisture forming at the tip. 'But I am not afraid.' She stroked him again, slowly. Then she moved her hips to press against his.

He closed his eyes and touched her breasts, rubbing the nipples with his thumbs as she held him between her legs, letting him feel how wet she was becoming. Then she teased herself with the head of his penis.

As she brought herself near to breaking again, his hands pressed harder on her breasts. Then he gave a sudden buck of his hips and pulled away from her hands, grabbing her by the waist, rolling her on to her back, pushing her legs apart. He was on top of her now, spreading the lips of her body and pushing inside her.

Without him having to urge her, she wrapped her legs around his waist, wanting to be even closer to him as he moved, lifting her head and begging for the kiss that would smother her cries.

He shook his head. 'I want to watch.' Then he raised himself on his hands to free his hips as he thrust.

She cried out as she had last night, and again, moaning as he moved faster. Then he slowed. 'Touch yourself,' he commanded. 'You know where.'

She slipped her hands between them, touching the place where they were joined before moving forward and giving herself up to pleasures that only increased at his answering thrusts. Then she reached her peak, tumbling down the other side of it, as his body tightened and then collapsed, limp on top of her.

He lay still for a moment. Then, he whispered, 'Why did I ever fight this? You are sublime.'

'I don't know,' she whispered back. 'You are usually so intelligent.'

He laughed and rolled off her. 'Now that it has been done, I do not think we will make matters any worse by doing it again. After a little rest, of course.'

'How little?' she asked.

He laughed again, rolled her on her side and gathered her to him, her back against his chest, grinding his hips against her. 'You will feel when I am ready, you wicked girl.' Then he kissed the side of her neck. 'But there is no reason to rush. We have all night.'

'Yes.' She sighed, smiling into the darkness ahead of her.

And the darkness smiled back. As she stared at the bedside table a foot from her face, she saw the outline of the little miniature propped against the candle stand and the perfect white smile of the lovely Prudence.

She stiffened in his arms.

'Cold?' he murmured. 'Let me keep you warm.'

'Yes,' she replied, shivering. Then she turned in his arms until she could see nothing but him.

Chapter Sixteen

A man could get used to this.

Miles stretched his feet to their fullest length, enjoying the way his toes did not poke out from under the covers or extend past the edge of the mattress. Then he threw his arms wide and did the same.

It was likely no bigger than the bed he'd rented at the Clarendon in London. That had been soft and clean, as well.

But here, the bed was exceptional. Not just clean, but pristine, pressed flat as paper and just as white. The hangings were purple velvet, the coverlet silk brocade. He felt like the King that had given the suite its name.

At the movement of his body, the heavy linen of the sheets rubbed his naked skin in a way that was as decadent as the kisses he had received last night. If he had not taken the lady back to her room, she'd be waking beside him and they'd have made love again. Then he'd have called for the servants to bring breakfast on a tray, so they could refresh themselves and make love once more.

Since this was his fantasy, he substituted the shirred eggs, fish, muffins and strong, black tea that they'd been feeding him for johnnycakes with maple syrup, black coffee and Kentucky corn whisky. He could imagine the taste of them, heavy sweetness and the grit of cornmeal. The taste of the liquor, both sharp and smooth. The smell of pine forests and the gulls screaming over the Delaware. There was so much about home that he missed: the newness of it all, the rough edges and the feeling of a world to conquer, just a few miles to the west.

But what use had he for the frontier? He forced himself to get out of the bed, stretching in the chill bedroom air and glancing out the window. The phrase, 'master of all he surveyed', popped into his head. Until this week, it had been nothing more than an expression. Suddenly, it was true. He had been reminded by the Prince Regent himself that though, technically, the land belonged to the Crown, he was responsible for the care of every inch of the property he could see, all the way to the horizon.

The staggering weight of the responsibility hit him again, as it did almost every morning, spoiling the glow of happiness. He wanted to crawl back between those delightful-smelling sheets, pull them over his head and refuse to come out. The men who had slept here before him had been birthed on clean white sheets, swaddled in silk and lace, and walked every step of their lives in well-heeled, bespoke boots until their inert body was arrayed on the satin pillow of their casket. And yet, when it had come to taking care of this place, they had failed.

Of course, they did not have his sense of vision. And they had not had Charity Strickland to help them. He grinned. She had called him brilliant. He did not like to think of himself as such. But Charity had been quite adamant about it. She had grown misty-eyed talking, listing his accomplishments in a way she had not when complimenting his looks.

That had been either his making or his undoing. She had not said she loved him in so many words. But she must have felt something very like that. She had looked at him last night as if he was the finest man on earth.

Then she had let him love her. And at some point, the room they'd shared had become the paradise he'd awakened in. Her perfume on the rumpled sheets had scented his dreams. Her kisses had filled his heart with uncontainable joy.

He had told her they would know in the morning if it had been a mistake. It was not. With such a woman at his side, the future might not be hopeless after all. He could share his life with her, his failures as well as his successes, and have no fear that she would turn from him, looking for a man who offered more.

It was not until he had walked to the basin for a wash and a shave that he looked in the mirror and remembered that he had shared nothing with her. She did not even know his name. What had possessed him to let the lie go on so long? Why had he come here in the first place? If he'd meant to hide, he'd done it in the first place anyone would look.

It had been because he had not really wanted to go. It was too late to call back the letter he'd sent to Pru, promising that he would return to marry her. Nor could Ed return from beyond to release him from the promise he had made to care for her. But if he was as smart as Charity seemed to think, he should be able to free himself from the trap Pru had set.

She had been quick enough to call him aimless when Ed had been alive, continually reminding him that he was a ne'er-do-well and not half the man his older brother was.

Her tune had changed immediately after the letter from England had arrived. It was some comfort to know that he had been clever enough to resist, when she had tried to seduce him before he'd left. Then, she had called his sense of honour naïve. In getting herself with child, she had found a way to use it to her advantage.

Perhaps he was naïve. He had offered to return and marry her because it was the right thing to do, comforting himself that he would be walking away from a world of trouble here in England. Perhaps he would not be lord of the manor, but he had barely begun to see what he might make of himself in America, where a man might count himself rich if he had a little money and a pretty wife.

He glanced at the miniature that was lying on the night table where he had dropped it on undressing the night before. Then he opened the drawer of the table and swept it out of sight. The little ivory oval had felt heavy as a millstone for some time. It was as lovely to look at as the woman who'd posed for it. But neither it nor she made him feel the way he did when he looked at Charity Strickland.

She was what he needed now. He needed her wisdom as well as her love. He did not like being Comstock any more than she wanted to be his Countess, but he could not help who he was. He would tell her everything that had happened, from the moment he had received the life-changing letter telling him he must come to England. He would apologise for lying to her. He would tell her of his love.

Then he would let her choose his fate. He would stay or go on her command. If she thought it right that he should marry Pru, he would do so. If not?

He grinned. He would offer for her. For her, he would be Comstock or plain, old Miles Strickland, or spend the rest of his life as Augustus Potts, if that was what she preferred. And he would do it all on the continent of her choosing. He would be and do whoever and whatever it took to give her the life she deserved.

By the way he felt after making it, he was sure that his decision was the right one. He was still poor, of course. And his life was still a disaster. But with the love of a good woman and a decent breakfast in him, he was one step closer to conquering the world.

He grinned at the servant coming down the hall towards him, full of the bonhomie that came the morning after the best night of his life. As the fellow drew closer, Miles had only a moment to wonder at the fact that he had not seen the man since the first day, when he'd taken the reins of the big black horse that had brought him here and walked it towards the stables. What was a groom doing in the guest wing of the main house?

The groom smiled back at him in reassurance, revealing a set of huge teeth that would have been worthy of his charges. Then, without a word of greeting, he pulled back his fist and drove it into Miles's stomach.

All the wind in his body left in one woof and there was an agonising moment where he was convinced that it would never return. But through his distress, he felt the big hand of the groom cupped around the back of his neck, keeping him from collapse.

'There, there, Mr Potts. It will pass.' He added a thunderous clap on the back, which sent the air rushing back into his lungs.

Miles looked up at the man through streaming eyes, still unable to speak.

The groom grinned. 'I was sent by the rest of the staff to give you that message.'

'Huh?' He attempted a response, but could manage nothing more than a wheeze.

'Perhaps things are different in America. But when you are in service, it is never wise to give yourself airs and behave like a member of the family, eating in the dining room and swanning about the house as if it is yer own.'

He could feel the first flame of anger, kindling behind the pain in his gut. He was the first to admit to his faults. But he had never *swanned* in his life. When he got his breath back, he was going to fill his gloves with scrap iron and give this fellow a lesson behind the stables on what was and was not *swanning.* But at the moment, all he could do was look up at him, eyes streaming from the pain.

The man allowed a few moments of silence to let his words sink in before continuing. 'Perhaps an auditor is a different kind of animal from a common servant, so we will let it pass.'

Miles opened his mouth to bellow that he was no kind of servant at all. He was the Eighth Earl of Comstock. And though he had not yet had time to investigate the cellars of his new home, there had been something on one of the older house plans that had looked rather like a dungeon. Unless this lout wanted to find himself locked in it, he had best return to the stables, where he belonged.

And then he stopped. He was still Potts until he had spoken to Charity. This was even worse than the gossip spreading after his visit to the village. The only thing that would be worse than lying to her would be having her hear the truth from someone else. So he closed his mouth and took the punishment he deserved.

The groom stooped to look him in the eye, his breath smelling of this morning's sausage and last night's sour ale. 'Whatever the Earl intends for you, I doubt it is to take liberties with his hospitality. I am sure he would not approve of anyone who would do harm to Miss Charity. Neither would we. We have known her since she was a wee girl, ya see?'

Miles's nod turned into a wince as the meaty hand on his shoulder tightened to pinch a nerve.

'And if a stranger should court her without honourable intentions?' He shrugged and gave a sad look. 'I would not want to be that fellow. And that is all I will say.'

'I understand,' Miles wheezed. 'No harm will come to her, on my life.'

'That is an excellent thing to swear on,' the groom said, with another smile, giving him a slap on the back that nearly sent him through the plaster on the opposite wall. 'For that is exactly what is at risk. Do you understand me?'

Miles nodded again.

'And if I was you I'd pack my bags right smartish and be on my way before something unfortunate happened.'

Probably something involving a hammer. Miles nodded again.

The groom nodded back to signify a bargain, then continued down the hall, whistling as if nothing had occurred.

Now that he was not being held upright, Miles slumped against the wall, taking shallow breaths until the pain began to ease. This was what came of telling lies and not appreciating rank, even when it was forced upon a fellow. An earl could get up to whatever dubious behaviour he chose and face no consequences. But the fictional Augustus Potts had no such magic shield and he had best watch his back until Charity had accepted his suit.

He dragged himself to his feet and wobbled down the stairs towards breakfast. Ready or not, the time had come to explain everything to Charity and throw himself on her mercy. Her anger was formidable, but a small thing when weighted against the risk that his own servants would beat him senseless to protect her.

But when he arrived at the ground floor, he changed his mind. Gregory Drake stood in the doorway, offering his coat to the butler. At the sight of Miles on the stairs, he smiled. Then his mouth opened, ready to speak.

Still too soon.

Could he not at least make it to the breakfast table before all hell broke loose?

'My…' Drake's greeting had already begun. In another second, the title would be out of his mouth and the shocked butler would be running to the basement to tell the staff. The whole house would know in the time it took him to find Charity and explain.

Miles jumped the last few steps to the floor, reaching for the fellow's arm as he spoke. 'Mr Drake! There is an urgent matter I must speak to you about concerning the entail.' He continued forward, pushing Charity's brother-in-law back through the open door, shutting it behind them and leaving them both coatless in the early-morning air.

'What the devil…?' Greg Drake stopped, probably remembering that, no matter how mad he appeared, one did not speak disrespectfully to a member of the peerage. 'My Lord Comstock—'

'Until I tell you otherwise, I am no such thing,' Miles interrupted. 'Not to you, or to anyone who might be with you.'

'I am alone,' Drake replied in confusion. 'For the moment, at least. I was in the mood for a gallop and set off on horseback at dawn. But Faith's husband, James Leggett, is just behind me. Our wives will be arriving by carriage later this morning with the servants and the luggage. When the girls heard that you'd left London, they insisted that we come to the country to welcome the heir.'

'God's teeth.' Miles cast a quick look at the closed door, hoping his outburst could not be heard though it. 'You must intercept them immediately. There is a problem.'

'Not with Miss Charity,' Drake said in alarm. 'Tell me she had not fallen ill.'

'Her health is excellent,' Miles replied. 'But... There has been a misunderstanding.'

'Charity misunderstood something?' A slow grin spread across the other man's face. 'That cannot be possible. Charity Strickland does not make mistakes. She knows more than the rest of the family put together.'

'Well, my identity is the one thing she is not aware of,' Miles snapped. 'She thinks I am an auditor named Augustus Potts.'

Drake was staring at him as though he had suddenly gone mad, which was quite possibly the case. 'Where did she get such a ridiculous idea?'

'From me.' There was no way he could imagine to explain the pass that he had come to, but he did his best. 'Things between Charity and myself are at a rather delicate juncture,' he said, carefully.

'A juncture.' He watched as his former auditor and future brother-in-law jumped to the logical conclusion. 'With Charity.' His expression changed from amused to incredulous.

'That should not be a surprise.' Miles gave him a warning glare. 'It is what everyone in this country, from the Prince on down, has expected of me. But Charity does not expect it. In fact, she would be four-square against marrying me if she knew I was Comstock.'

'Would she consider marrying Mr Potts?' Drake said with raised eyebrows.

'It doesn't matter whether she would or not,' Miles said. 'Mr Potts does not exist.'

'And which of you sent me this letter?' Drake asked, pulling the note Miles had sent him from a coat pocket.

'Let us say that it was from both of me,' Miles replied.

Drake nodded. 'Then I think it is wise that we blame it on Mr Potts. I have come to tell him that it is not legal to distribute pornography in England and the Earl of Comstock wants nothing to do with it.'

'It is not legal in America, either,' Miles answered. 'But I did not ask about the legality. I asked how it could be done. The items in question were obviously meant for someone's private enjoyment and were never intended to be part of the Comstock estate. They are too valuable to destroy. And I...or rather, Mr Potts cannot exactly hawk them on a street corner.'

'Then, tell Mr Potts that I have the necessary contacts to make it happen and an estimate of the amount of money he is likely to receive should a discreet sale take place. I am ready to act, at your convenience.'

Miles glanced at the numbers on the paper and smiled. 'That is exactly what I'd hoped to hear. We will begin this afternoon.'

The ever-efficient Drake reached into another pocket and produced a stack of letters and handed them to Miles. 'I have brought your mail from London, as well. You received letters on the last two ships from America.' He turned to look, as a horse and rider came galloping up the drive. 'And this is James Leggett, just arriving. Since I am not sure which name you wish to use, let us spare you the awkwardness of an introduction. If you go back into the house, Mr Potts, I will explain matters to him, so he might ride back and inform the ladies.'

'And I will go and talk to Charity,' Miles said, with a sigh of relief. 'The matter will most likely be settled by the time you arrive at the house. Even so, proceed with caution and give nothing away until I tell you to.'

'Very good.' Drake strode out to meet his approaching brother-in-law and Miles returned to the house, walking past the surprised butler, who was watching him with suspicion.

'Confidential business for Lord Comstock,' Miles

said, giving him an arch look in return that dared him to enquire further.

Then he went off to find Charity, before the fellow could summon a pair of stout footmen to beat an explanation out of him.

Chapter Seventeen

Charity awoke the next morning in her own bed, unsure of how she had got there. A vague memory surfaced of being wrapped in her dressing gown and carried down the hall, then tucked safely into her own bed with a final kiss. As he had walked, he'd whispered in her ear of the importance of being found where she was expected when her maid arrived.

She had nodded sleepily and pressed kisses on to his bare chest, still not ready to let him go.

In response, he had groaned and muttered something about her need to recognise that even a virile man needed his rest and that virgins were supposed to be easily satisfied, not insatiable.

She smiled. After last night, the word did not apply to her. Then the smile faded.

When she had gone to his room, she had thought that what they were doing was to be an isolated incident. It would be a final goodbye and the memory of it would act as bulwark against an uncertain future. Now that it had happened, she could not stop imagining a repeat of last night's activities, as soon as she felt sufficiently refreshed.

Then she remembered all the reasons she should not. Potts had made it clear from the first that he wanted to return to America and had not wavered on that point in any of their conversations. He had a fiancée and slept with her picture beside his bed. Even now, he might be waking to see Prudence smiling back at him from that miniature and regretting his weakness of last night.

Worse yet, he might already be gone. The fact that Charity was in love with him made no difference. She had found him too late.

But at least she had found him. The idea that he might love her in return had been a foolish one, of course. He was far too perfect for that. But if she had wanted to experience the kind of passionate affair normally denied to proper young ladies, he had been a perfect choice. He had taken her to paradise. Now he meant to disappear. She need never fear seeing him walking on Bond Street with another woman's children or be forced to make nice to his lovely wife at some inescapable social gathering. She would have perfect memories, nothing more.

It was what she'd told him she wanted. But what if she'd changed her mind? As she'd slept, when her mind was unfettered from common sense, she had dreamed of a long sea voyage and a ship pulling into a strange harbour. It had looked as she'd imagined his country looked, roughhewn, bustling with strangers and Red Indians. But there had been a familiar face waiting for her in the crowd on the dock. Potts had waved and smiled, and held his arms out to her as she had walked down the gangplank.

Her dream might have been more accurate had she imagined the lady from the miniature standing at his side. For it was probable that he would marry Prudence the moment he returned.

It did not matter what Charity might want or dream. She could not have him. In truth, she would not know what to do with him, even if she caught him. She had always assumed that a plain woman would end up with a plain husband. But seeing Potts disrobed last night had done nothing to dissuade her opinion that he was a god walking the earth. He was handsome, intelligent and when they were alone, he demonstrated skills that had nothing to do with auditing.

When Dill entered, to prepare her for the day, the maid took one look at her and her mouth fell open in amazement. Then it snapped closed in a catlike grin. 'A bath this morning, miss? They can be very soothing on the muscles.' It seemed she had found one thing that her normally obtuse maid understood completely.

'Why would I…?' Charity said slowly. She glanced in the mirror. Then pulled on her spectacles and looked again. Of course, Dill had guessed what had happened. She had felt beautiful last night. Though she had not thought it to be true, emotions must have a profound effect on physical appearance.

She was still not as pretty as her sisters. They had been exceptionally beautiful, even before falling in love. But she could not deny that, this morning, she was radiant. She looked like Hope had been after a week with Mr Drake. She looked as Faith had when Mr Leggett had changed her life. She had promised that nothing would change after.

But clearly, she had fallen in love.

She looked back at her maid, unrepentant, mind racing to find a course of action. 'No bath, Dill. There will not be time to heat the water. Mr Potts plans to leave today. I need to speak with him while he is still here. How quickly can you dress me?'

Dill looked at her, considering. 'An hour, at least.' She pulled a confection of ribbons and lace from the wardrobe, draping it over her hand.

Suddenly, there was a knock on the door and what sounded like the housekeeper, trying to console an increasingly emotional parlour maid.

'Come in,' Charity called, baffled at what would have them up in arms so early in the morning.

'Miss Charity.' The woman bobbed a nervous curtsy, while the maid cowered behind her. 'We have just come from the dining room.'

'Yes, Mrs Till?' The information was not surprising in the least.

'It is Millie's job to polish the silver. When she opened the sideboard, she discovered a significant absence.'

Charity's mind returned to Potts's threat of the previous day. 'Indeed.'

'A dozen spoons, fifteen forks and two pair of short candlesticks,' Mrs Till affirmed.

'It wasn't me, miss. I told her as soon as I found them missing. It wasn't me.'

'Of course not, Millie,' Charity said, smiling at the girl to calm her. 'I do not suspect you or any of the servants.'

'Thank you, miss.' The girl sagged with relief.

Charity turned back to Mrs Till. 'Do not worry about the matter. I will settle it all when I come down to breakfast.'

'Very good, miss.'

Charity thought for a moment, and then smiled. 'And do you happen to know if Mr Potts has gone, yet?'

'I saw him in the main hall a few moments ago,' the housekeeper said.

'Speak to Chilson for me. Tell him that Potts is not to leave until I have spoken to him.'

'Of course, miss.' With another curtsy, the housekeeper turned, shooing the maid back out of the bedroom and closing the door behind them.

Then Charity turned back to her maid. 'I have changed my mind, Dill. I would definitely enjoy a bath. Take all the care you wish with my hair and leave no ribbon unpressed. This morning, I need to be as close to perfection as you can bring me.'

'Yes, miss.' If Dill was surprised at the Herculean task set for her, she gave no indication. But Charity saw no other way forward. If one meant to stop the man one loved from marrying the wrong woman, one needed to look one's best.

When Miles could not find Charity in the library, he tried the breakfast room. But though it was almost half past nine, there was no indication that she had eaten so much as a slice of toast. Nor was she in the study, the morning room, or several other sitting rooms that he had discovered while searching the ground floor.

She was likely still in her bedroom.

Since a gentleman should not even know where that was, he was none too eager to search her out there. The warning he had got from the groom was still fresh in his memory and the bruise from it was still blossoming on his stomach. He did not want to risk a second lesson before the staff learned his identity. But they might never know if he did not find Charity to tell her. There was nowhere left to look but her room.

As he started towards the stairs, he heard a scrabbling in the upper hallway and saw Pepper appear above him. If possible, the dog looked even angrier than usual, possibly because of the offence done to his canine dignity. His collar had been decked with more ribbons than a maypole. After a single bark of warning he then pelted down the stairs straight for him and used the advantage of his elevation to leap from the fifth step, firing himself like a furry bullet at Miles's face.

He reached out and caught the dog in mid-air, leaving him suspended by the scruff of his neck in a cloud of rage and women's cologne. Then he brought the dog to eye level, staring into its little black eyes. 'Are we finished?'

There was no answer, of course, other than some angry squirming at being bested, again.

'I think we are. Like it or not, dog, if your mistress can abide me, I mean to stay and there is nothing you can do about it. But there will be some advantages.'

He reached out and untied the ribbons, dropping them to the floor. Then he set the dog back on the ground, where it gave a shake of relief, followed by a prodigious sneeze.

He stared down at it. 'You are right. It smells much better on her than it does on you. I recommend you find something foul to roll in. You will feel worlds better, afterwards.' He reached in his pocket for the muffin he had filched on his recent pass through the breakfast room and dropped it on the floor. 'You need this more than I do. And I need to find Charity. If you still hate me, do not bother to attack again until this afternoon.'

He started up the stairs again. He had almost gained the landing when he heard the sound of footsteps, thundering up the flight behind him. It took effort to prevent himself from running and to remind himself that the best way to appear innocent was to make an effort not to look guilty. Instead of panicking, he stepped to the side and gripped the banister, preparing to let the person or persons pass him.

His plan failed, utterly. A pair of hands hit him square between the shoulders, dislodging his grip on the rail and pushing him forward. Before he could fall he was caught again by two sets of hands, one on each bicep. The men who had him lifted him easily to his feet and further, carrying him the rest of the way up the stairs with his suspended feet slapping helplessly against the risers.

He glanced to one side and saw the groom that had accosted him earlier. 'You again.' On his other side was an equally large footman. 'And this time, you have brought a friend. It has only been a few minutes since our last meeting. What is it that you think I have done between now and then?'

'Pinched m'lord's spoons,' the groom replied with a toothy grin as if he had been waiting his whole life for an opportunity like this one.

'Now, see here.' Then he realised that he had no idea how to answer a charge that was, technically, true. 'I am sure, if we find Miss Strickland and discuss the matter, she will tell you that this is an honest mistake. Drastic action is not necessary.'

'She knows,' the footman grunted. 'We were told that we were to detain you.'

'I do not think that is what she meant,' he said, only to realise that he had no idea what her intentions had been. If she had discovered he was Comstock, it was exactly the sort of thing she might do, only to offer a false apology and claim that she'd had no idea since he had not bothered to tell the truth. In fact, the longer he thought of it, the more likely it was that this was exactly what had happened.

He struggled in their grip, trying and failing to break free. 'Now, see here, fellows. You are making a terrible mistake.'

'It's you what made the mistake,' said the groom. 'But you can't say you weren't warned.'

They had reached the top of the stairs now and were hauling him forward into the old wing, towards places that were all but abandoned.

'You would not be doing this if you knew who I was,' he insisted.

'Yer Mr Potts.'

'That is who I claimed to be,' he admitted. 'But my real name is Miles Strickland.'

The footman's hands tightened on his arm and the groom let out a braying laugh.

'Truly,' he insisted. 'I am the heir to the title, the Earl of Comstock come from America.'

'And I'm the Queen of Spain,' the footman announced, making the groom laugh again.

'If you let me go, I will prove it. I have the Earl's signet in my room.'

'Next to the soup spoons,' the footman replied.

'Probably stole the signet, too,' the groom agreed. 'Cannot trust Americans. My uncle was at the Battle of Trenton.'

'Do not think you can hold me responsible for that,' Miles argued. 'It happened before I was born.'

They had reached the end of the first old hallway and his captors turned right, continuing down the next hall until they were far out of earshot from anyone in the main part of the house. At the end of the hall, a door was standing open, as if waiting for him. Miles swung his legs forward, trying to find purchase against rug, or wall, or anything that might stop their progress. 'This is all an honest mistake and I do not mean to punish you for what you have done to me.'

This was greeted with even more laughter.

'I am sure, if you take me to Charity, this will be sorted out in no time.'

'Charity, is it?' Without warning, the groom released his arm and he dropped to the rug, barely able to keep his feet. This unsteadiness worked to his advantage, for the blow that struck his chin did not land with the catastrophic force the groom had intended. But it was more than enough to daze him as he was pushed into an empty bedroom whose only distinguishing feature was the size of the lock on the door. Before he could rouse himself sufficiently to argue, the door had slammed and he heard the bolt hit home, trapping him inside.

Chapter Eighteen

When Dill had finished with her ministrations, Charity examined herself in the mirror. She had never considered herself a vain creature. But today, she had to admit that she had never looked better. The spectacles rather spoiled her attempt at conventional beauty. But so would squinting, which she would most certainly do if she tried to do without her glasses.

Since she had never been at a loss for words before, it was most unexpected that her near-complete transformation into a proper young lady had been easier than coming up with an argument that would convince Potts to stay. Far too much of her position seemed to hinge on the fact that he should not go because she could not bear to part with him. Since this was exactly the opposite of what she had promised, she was not even sure if she should announce the fact.

Other points in her favour included the fact that Prudence was a conniving hussy who was in no way worthy of him. Until he arrived in Philadelphia, he could not even be sure that she had told the truth about her pregnancy. Should it be a lie, he might be trapped there by finances and unable to return even though he wanted to.

Unless he could definitively demonstrate the existence of the afterlife, there was no proof that his brother would know whether he had kept the promise or not. Nor could they be sure that his brother would expect him to abide by it in the current circumstances.

Only after she had made these points did she want to resort to the fact that she loved him. The rational voice in her head insisted that it was the lowest form of debate to appeal to emotion if there were facts to support the argument. But for the first time in her life, there was another voice demanding that she follow her heart and do it quickly before she lost the chance.

That was assuming it was not too late already. When she reached the ground floor, there was no sign of Potts in the breakfast room, the study, the library or any of the other rooms she could think to check. With growing trepidation, she rushed back up the stairs to the Tudor room.

It was empty. The bed was still rumpled from last night's activities. But the wardrobe was open and empty, as were the drawers. There was no sign of the leather satchel she had noticed on a chair, last night. Like a coward, she had taken too long in preparing to meet him. Or perhaps the staff had not got her message to prevent him from leaving.

Maybe it had been too late from the start. He was an early riser who could have been gone at first light.

But she had refused to believe that he would go without at least saying farewell.

There was only one place left to look. If his horse was no longer in the stable, she would know that it was too late. She should hurry, since there might still be a chance to stop him. But as she left his room to head to the door, it felt as if she was slogging through mud. Each step grew more difficult because she was afraid of what she would find.

But as she came down the main stairs, she heard the sound of people talking and laughing in the hall, and Pepper running in circles on the parquet and barking furiously at visitors.

'Charity!' Hope was waiting in the entrance hall, arms out to embrace her. Right behind was her oldest sister, Faith. Beside them in an animated conversation with each other were their two husbands.

'I have missed you,' she said, coming down the stairs to hug them both. The words were true. Though she had been waiting a lifetime for them to leave home and stop pestering her, their actual departure had left her lonelier than she'd expected. But now, when she assumed she would be joyful at their return, she felt nothing but numb. Since they'd been gone, her entire life had changed and she had no idea what to say about it. 'It has been so long.'

'Only a few weeks,' Faith said, kissing her on the cheek.

'And now that the Earl is here, we do not have to worry that you will be alone,' Hope said with a smile.

Charity looked past them at the open door, but saw

no sign of the peer. 'I have been told he was in the village, yesterday. But I have seen no sign of him as yet. Is he arriving after you?'

'He is not here yet?' Faith said, giving their sister an odd look.

'My mistake,' Hope said, quickly.

'He is not here yet,' Faith repeated somewhat more loudly, to catch the attention of her husband.

'How strange,' Mr Leggett replied, frowning at Mr Drake.

'Truly,' Hope repeated. Then she glanced at her husband, as well. 'You said he was going to settle things before we arrived.'

James Leggett glared at him, as well. 'You said matters would be settled by the time we arrived.'

'I thought they would.' Gregory Drake's brow furrowed. 'But obviously not.' Then he looked to Charity. 'Perhaps Mr Potts can explain matters to us.'

'You know about Potts?' she said, surprised.

'The Earl told Gregory all about him,' Hope supplied. 'We thought one of them would be here to meet us.' She frowned again. 'We hoped it would be the Earl.'

The assembled party was looking at her now, as if expecting her to produce one man or the other from under her skirts.

'I believe you have just missed Potts,' she said, forcing herself to smile as if his departure did not matter to her at all.

This was met by a sea of blank faces and more expectant silence.

'He left early this morning,' she added. 'He was already gone when I came down for breakfast.' It was surprisingly difficult to voice her fears aloud. Her tone sounded rather like she was about to cry.

'Where did he go?' Faith asked, arms crossed.

'He has spoken more than once of returning to America when he was through here. I believe his home is in Philadelphia.' She blinked at them, waiting for them to lose interest and go back to worrying about the Earl, as they had been for the last three months. It was not as if she would be able to forget Potts. But perhaps if there was something to distract her, it might not be quite so painful to remember him.

Her sisters shot cryptic glances at their husbands. Then, Faith said, 'Perhaps there is a servant who can give us more information on his plans.'

All the servants would want to talk about was the missing silver. The whole family would have the wrong opinion of him if she did not make it clear to Chilson that the auditor had got her permission to remove the items. 'You are right. Asking the servants is an excellent idea,' Charity said. 'I will go and talk to them immediately.'

'Oh, darling, do not bother yourself,' Hope said, standing between her and escape. 'Gregory and James will make the necessary enquiries.'

Before she could think of another excuse, her sisters had linked their arms in hers and were leading her towards the stairs. 'Come along, dearest,' Faith said. 'It has been ages since we have talked. You must tell us how you have been managing.' Then, under the guise of devotion, they dragged her up the stairs and towards her bedchamber.

'It has not been so very long,' Charity said, trying to struggle free. 'And nothing at all has happened here. Nothing at all.' If she meant to put them off the scent, her denial had been far too strenuous. She changed the subject. 'How was your honeymoon? Tell me all about Italy.'

'Never mind that. Tell us all about Mr Potts,' Hope said, with a feline smile.

'He is the auditor sent by the Earl,' Charity said.

'And?' Faith added.

This was very strange. The pair of them were acting as if they knew something they could not possibly know. Was the truth still plain on her face? Or was this just sisterly revenge, for the way she had tortured Hope when she had fallen in love with Mr Drake?

If so, it was unfair. Mr Drake was an Englishman and had lived just down the street from them. It was clear that they were meant for each other. It was not as if Hope had fallen in love with an engaged American.

She disengaged her arms from theirs, pushed her spectacles up the bridge of her nose and gave them her sternest look. 'There is nothing more to tell about Potts.'

They ignored her, pushing her into her bedroom and shutting the door.

'If there is nothing to tell, how do you explain your hair?' Faith said, snatching at a curl.

Charity slapped her hand away. 'Leave it be. There is nothing wrong with it.'

'Has Dill forgotten how to braid it in that ghastly coronet you favoured?'

Ghastly? Had it really been so bad? 'I requested a change,' Charity said.

'Curls,' Hope said with an ecstatic sigh. 'I always knew you would look better with them.'

'Indeed,' Faith agreed. 'The mysterious Mr Potts has put a curl in our little sister's hair.'

'And colour in her cheeks,' Hope agreed. 'Not to mention the ruffles and lace on the rest of her. Mr Potts is a worker of miracles.'

'There is nothing miraculous about him,' she replied. 'Was nothing miraculous, I mean. He was an American hired by the Earl. And now he is gone.'

'Is he, really?' Hope said, raising her eyebrows.

Faith gestured to another gown still lying on the bed. 'Have you taken to changing for tea when you are in the house alone?'

'So what if I have?' Charity snapped. 'There is nothing unusual about it. Nor is there anything strange about the gown I am wearing. Hope chose them for me when we were in London.'

'And you refused to wear any of them,' Faith reminded her. 'But while we were gone, you have gone all ruffles and curls.'

Hope was rummaging through the wardrobe. 'Her dinner gowns smell of perfume. She has been wearing them.'

'Now that you have finally left me alone, I have been doing the things you've been badgering me to do all year.'

'For Mr Potts,' Faith said.

'He is a very interesting man,' she allowed.

'And very handsome,' Hope added.

'Not really,' Charity lied.

Hope looked at Faith and repeated, 'Very handsome.'

'You do not know him at all, so you cannot possibly make that assumption,' Charity said.

Faith ignored her logic and stared back at her. 'Never mind how much we know about him. How well do you know Mr Potts?'

Biblically.

The temptation to announce the fact was almost irresistible. Instead, she answered, 'He was here for several days. I was helping him with the audit.'

'And is it going well?' Hope asked. The question was innocent enough, but the meaning was something deeper.

'Of course,' Charity replied.

'Show it to us,' Faith said, arms folded.

'There is nothing written down,' she said, giving up the pretence.

'Then what have you been doing, all this time?' Hope said, smiling as if she knew.

'We have been searching for the missing Comstock diamonds,' she admitted.

'And?' Faith asked.

'Playing chess,' she added.

'And?' Hope asked.

'Billiards,' she concluded through gritted teeth.

Her sisters shared a look of sympathetic frustration. Then Faith said, 'If you were going to play games, I could recommend several that are even better than that.'

'We are not supposed to be encouraging her,' Hope reminded her.

'But I cannot think of a better match than…Mr Potts,' Faith said.

'But chess?' Hope shook her head. 'Gentlemen do not like to be bested by ladies.'

'He beat me,' Charity said, unable to keep from smiling at the memory.

Faith dropped into the chair by the vanity table, overcome with shock.

'He gave up three pieces, to start, and still he beat me.'

Hope sat on the edge of the bed, stunned to silence.

'And he has been willing to listen to my ideas about the estate,' she added. 'Not that it matters. I doubt he will have any influence at all over Comstock.'

'I would not be so sure,' Hope said faintly and received a quelling glare from Faith.

'Do not contradict your sister,' Faith said, as if either of them had ever cared what Charity thought. Then she turned with an overly bright smile. 'Suppose he decided to stay. If there was a position here on the estate and we could get him to return, would that please you?'

More than anything in the world. She should have run to find him the moment she awoke. 'What I want does not figure in the equation,' she said at last, a lump rising in her throat.

Hope clapped her hands together, as if a miracle

had occurred. 'You do want him to stay. Do not bother to deny it. And it is because you have fallen in love with him.'

At the suggestion, Faith looked equally overjoyed. 'I cannot think of a more perfect situation.'

'Then you are not thinking hard enough,' Charity snapped. 'England is probably full of men who would be more suitable than Potts.' And she did not want a single one of them.

'It is normal to have doubts,' Hope said.

Faith nodded in agreement. 'But the important thing is how he feels about you.'

'If she has been dressing for dinner, I am sure he is favourably disposed,' Hope said. 'Her gowns are scandalously low-cut.'

'Because you chose them for me,' Charity said, exasperated.

'Your bosom is your best feature,' Hope said and Faith nodded in agreement.

'My bosom is neither here nor there,' Charity concluded.

'To you, perhaps,' Hope said. 'But I dare say the gentleman you dined with has noticed it.'

'She is blushing,' Faith said, eyes narrowed as if it helped her see the truth.

'One might even say you are glowing,' Hope added.

'Has he offered yet?' Faith said.

'Not to me.'

'I am sure it is only a matter of time,' Hope said. 'He was probably waiting until the family arrived so he might surprise us.'

'I think we have had surprises enough already,' Faith reminded her. 'We are all familiar with the mischief that happens when men and women in love are left alone together, but I never expected it of Charity.'

'We are not in love,' Charity insisted. Of course, she knew what she felt for him. But she had not managed to say it out loud and he had done nothing to make her think the statement would be reciprocated.

'If you do not think that is what has happened here, then you are more naïve than I thought possible,' Faith said, with the superior air of an older sister. 'Mr Potts will be staying, whether you expect him to or not. And, after what has happened between you, we all expect an offer to be forthcoming.'

'Do not make us summon Grandmama,' Hope said. 'She talks a good game when it comes to liberal behaviour. But that will change immediately once she has seen the two of you together.'

'We are not likely to be together, ever again,' Charity insisted. 'Even if we were, I do not want my family forcing him into an offer that he does not wish to make.'

For a moment, her sisters stared at her in silence. Then both tried to talk at once. 'Why ever not? Is there another gentleman? Are you waiting for someone? What possessed you?'

The questions were coming faster than she could answer. She held up a hand to halt them.

'We discussed the matter between us, before we began. We had agreement.' And yet she had been ready to break it as soon as it was time for him to go.

'An agreement not to marry?' Faith practically shouted at her. 'Then we have been misled. The man is no gentleman.'

Hope reached out quickly, glancing towards the hall as if afraid that someone might hear. 'Now, Sister. Let us not jump to conclusions on his motives. He is not here to question.'

Then she smiled at Charity with false brilliance. 'But since Charity is involved, I am sure that there is a perfectly logical explanation as to why we should not start gathering orange blossoms. Is there another man involved? Are you waiting to meet the Earl of Comstock, perhaps?'

At this, Charity laughed aloud. 'Whatever gave you such a daft idea?'

'There is nothing daft about the notion of marrying our American cousin,' Hope said.

'Of course you would say so. You wished to marry him yourself,' Charity reminded her.

'And then I met Mr Drake,' Hope said. 'But if there had not been Gregory, I would not have minded overly, settling for Miles Strickland.'

'And he is the last man on earth I would want to marry.'

'It is unfair of you to judge the man before you have even met him,' Faith said.

'He might be just the sort of fellow to suit you,' Hope added.

'Or he might be exactly like our grandfather was,' Charity reminded her.

'Grandfather was not so very bad,' Faith demurred.

'To you, perhaps. But that was because you agreed with him. He locked me out of the library and threatened to give the books away, since they made me unmanageable.'

'They were only threats,' Hope reminded her. 'The library is as complete as it ever was.'

'You were lucky that he was not the sort to result to violence,' Faith said. 'Since he was the head of the family, he had a right to discipline the children in his house however he saw fit.'

'He could have whipped me from now until judgement. But that would not have changed the fact that I was right and he was wrong,' Charity declared. 'If he had listened to any of my suggestions, we might not be in the mess we are in.'

'You must be sure to inform the new Earl of the fact, when we manage to find him,' Hope said, smiling.

There was a sharp rap on the door and the sound of muttering male voices in the hall.

Without waiting for Charity's permission, Faith opened it and let her husband and Mr Drake into the room.

'There is no sign of him,' Mr Leggett said. 'His horse is still in the stable and the stable boys know nothing about any proposed trip.'

'I spoke to Chilson, who is beside himself with worry,' Drake supplied. 'Apparently, there was an altercation in the hall today.'

'That is nonsense,' Charity insisted. The house had been quiet until her family had arrived, expecting to find the Earl. She and Potts had parted in silence, at dawn. The joyful noise made before that had been done in a wing empty of servants.

'A groom struck him,' Drake said, ignoring her interruption.

'For what reason?'

'It was at Chilson's instruction.' Mr Drake glanced at her and then back at her sisters. 'Since he cannot be found, the butler fears that the matter may have got out of hand. The groom has been summoned back to the house to explain what happened to him, after the attack.'

'Good Lord,' Leggett said, wiping his brow. 'He will have all of our heads.'

'If he is alive to do so,' Drake said glumly.

'Who are you talking about?' Charity interrupted.

'Comstock,' the two men said in unison.

'What reason would they have to strike the Earl?' she said, now truly baffled.

Mr Drake looked past her, to her sisters. 'Apparently, it was a matter of honour, involving Charity.'

Everyone stared at her, waiting for an explanation.

She stared back. 'I have no idea what could have given him such an idea. I have never met the new Comstock and he has done nothing to me that would result in the servants springing to my defence.'

There was another significant silence as the entire family stared at her.

Then Faith said, 'You have never met the Earl.'

'No,' she said again. 'I have not.' She had met another American instead. One who came from the same city and arrived at the same time that the villagers reported seeing the Earl. A man who had been as interested in finding the diamonds as he had been in understanding the running of the estate.

A man who had sat at her grandfather's desk as though he belonged there even though he did not look like an earl, or talk like an earl, or act like an earl. He had been far too reasonable to be a member of the peerage. Nor did he look anything like a member of the family. They had been through the portrait gallery from one end to the other and she had not seen a single part of him that looked as if his picture would end up hanging with the rest of them.

'Potts,' she said, still unable to believe it.

There was a knock on the door and Mr Leggett opened it and stepped out into the hall to question Hoover, the groom.

Faith shook her head in pity. 'It is Comstock's business why he would tell such an outlandish story. Or why he would involve us in deceiving you. But really, Charity, I have no idea why you would be so foolish as to believe him.'

He had lied to her from the very first moment he'd met her. If he could lie about a thing like his name, then there was no telling what the truth of the rest might be.

'Never mind that now, dear,' Hope said in a gentle tone. 'Can you tell us what has happened to him?'

'I have no idea.' Other than that the new Earl of Comstock might have run away to America leaving them all to fend for themselves.

'He is in a bedroom in the old wing,' Leggett said

from the doorway. 'The servants are under the impression that you wanted him detained until the magistrate could be called, for stealing the dining-room silver.'

'I said no such thing,' she insisted, feeling sorry for the mistake until she remembered the horrible trick that he had played on her. 'But if that is what happened to him, then I am glad of it. I do not care if he never gets out.'

'Are you forgetting that he is not some American nobody? He is the Earl of Comstock.' Mr Leggett appeared ready to shout at her for the utter stupidity of her behaviour. But his wife threw up a hand of warning and he fell silent.

'Show us,' Faith said to the groom.

'Oh, yes, Hoover,' Charity agreed. 'Take us to him so that I can say to his face what I said to you all, right now.'

As she walked, she heard the worried murmurs from her sisters as they dissected the story of her first love, creating a far more interesting version of it than the truth had been.

'Broken heart…'

'Poor dear…'

'Should have known better…'

She had a good mind to turn on them and give them a taste of what lay in store for Potts. Perhaps she should have been smart enough to see the truth. But she was sure that her heart had not been broken since she could hear the blood pounding in her ears with each step. He had made a fool of her. The whole family had, for they'd arrived at the house knowing exactly who he was, fully aware that she had no clue. Then, rather than telling her the truth, they had allowed her to go on in ignorance while they'd laughed at her.

Her sisters' whispers were far off the mark. But Mr Leggett had a far more accurate assessment. She distinctly heard him say something that ended with '…safer where he is.'

When she arrived at the place where the servants had imprisoned the perfidious Miles Strickland, she gave the door handle a rattle. 'Comstock!' She rattled again, but it did not want to give way. 'I have come back to give you what you deserve.'

When he did not answer, she shouted again, 'Comstock! You liar, open this door.'

Mr Drake put her gently to the side and tried the handle himself. When it did not give to his touch, he pulled a penknife from his pocket and thrust it into the gap between the door and frame. After a few moments' patient jiggling, there was a click as the bolt slid back and the door could be opened.

She lunged forward, ready to confront the Earl, only to be brought up short by her sisters grabbing her arms and pulling her back.

'Now, now, Charity,' Hope said softly. 'You must give the man a chance to recover.'

'He has nothing to recover from,' she said. The groom shuffled nervously from side to side as she struggled to break free. 'But he will once I get hold of him. He's had three days of chances to tell me the truth and has not taken any of them.'

Mr Drake opened the door, stuck his head into the

room and called, 'My lord?' Then he threw it wide and stepped into the room, coming out a moment later.

He looked at Hoover. 'Are you sure this was the room?'

The white-faced groom gave a solemn nod.

She yanked her arms free of sisterly restraint and went into the room. 'Do not try my patience further, Comstock. You owe me an explanation.' But there was no point in lecturing him.

She was talking to an empty room.

Chapter Nineteen

She had managed to lose the Earl of Comstock.

Actually, the servants had. But since everyone was convinced that they had done it at her behest, she was the one likely to be blamed for it.

Charity did not overly mind the fact. If hell had opened and swallowed him whole, he would have wholeheartedly deserved it. She could not exactly blame him for seducing her. That had been totally her idea. But she'd never have suggested it had she known who he was.

There was no reason to lie to her. Yet he had done it from the first moment to the last. If he had told her who he was and said he wanted to leave, she would have packed his bags and helped him go. Instead, he had lied.

The servants were searching the house, top to bottom, but had found no sign of him. She had told them of his habit of climbing down drainpipes, but the window of his prison had not had so much as a scrap of ivy to cling to. The door had been locked from the outside, just as the servants had left it. There was no obvious way out of the room.

Where had he gone?

'How could you?' Faith was still trying to scold her, as if it was somehow her fault that he was missing.

'It was not my idea,' she replied. 'I only wished to speak to him before he left. The blame lies with him. If he had done a better job of concealing his theft, then the staff would not have discovered it and assumed the worst. If he had waited where he was until someone came to let him out, we would have nothing to worry about now. And if he has come to some misadventure?' She shrugged, smiling.

She was sure he had not. He was not an idiot. He would turn up when he was ready. If she had cared to find him, she might have applied herself to the problem, for it was an interesting question. If they did not find him in a day or so, perhaps she would look.

'You are incorrigible,' Faith whispered.

'Quite possibly,' Charity said, feeling somewhat better. There might be curls in her hair and she was developing a penchant for frilly dresses, but it was a relief to know that three days with Potts had not improved her personality. 'I am going to the library,' she said with a smile. 'Call me when they find the body.'

But when she arrived in her favourite room of the house, it was already occupied. Mr Drake had set two large wooden crates on the biggest of the library tables and was staring at the shelves as if trying to find the best place to start.

'What are you doing?' She stood in the doorway, frozen in shock.

Mr Drake looked up at her with the professional smile he had used when solving other people's problems. 'Business for Comstock.'

'What sort of business, precisely?'

'Nothing you need worry about,' he said, still smiling.

'Indulge me,' she said, her throat tightening in panic.

'Comstock has decided to sell off part of the collection to make up the deficiency in his finances.'

'No.' Where she had felt hot with rage on learning of his lies, this final betrayal left her feeling ice cold inside.

'He did not tell you?' Mr Drake's smile flickered for a moment and his eyes were sympathetic.

She shook her head.

'If you ask him when he returns, I am sure he will explain it to you,' he said. 'However, it is not really my place to do so.'

'Because you work for him,' she said. It was as she had feared from the first. He had barely arrived, and yet, Comstock had already begun to turn the family against her.

'He wants what is best for you, I'm sure.'

'So did my grandfather,' she said. Just as she'd always feared, though Miles Strickland was young and handsome, at heart he was no different than the last Earl.

She needed an intercessor. Someone to stop this until she could find a way to protect the books. 'Hope!'

She turned and ran back to the front hall where her sisters and Mr Leggett were conferring with the servant. 'Hope!' She grabbed her sister by the arm, tugging on her sleeve as she had when she was a little girl, unable to control the panic she felt at the changes that had taken place in their lives. 'Hope.'

Her sister stopped. 'What do you need, Charity?'

If anyone could reason with Mr Drake on the disposition of the books, it was his wife. 'Your husband is crating up the library,' she said. 'My library,' she added. 'Make him stop.'

Mr Drake had followed her back from the library and gave his wife a helpless shrug. 'I am acting on the instruction of Comstock. We discussed the disposal of certain items.'

Hope looked back at her sister. 'As we have been trying to tell you for years, Charity, it is not your library. It is Comstock's. He can do what he wants with it. If you have a problem with that, you must take it up with him.'

'But to do that, we must find him,' Faith reminded her. 'And since you have caused the problem…'

'For the last time—'

Suddenly, there was a clattering in the wall as if several pounds of stones had been dropped from a great height.

The family turned in every direction. Looking about them for the source of the sound.

In the quiet that followed, they heard a man's moan.

'This house is not haunted, is it?' Mr Leggett said doubtfully.

'Do not be ridiculous,' Charity snapped. 'There are no such things as spirits.'

'If any place has ghosts, I would expect it would be this one,' Mr Drake said. 'It is large enough to hold several.'

Now there came a strange, syncopated scrabbling that grew louder as if it was approaching, though nothing could be seen in either of the halls.

And then there was a bark.

'It is just Pepper,' she said with an annoyed sigh. 'He is chasing something through the walls. Although how he found his way inside them, I have no idea.'

'The more important question should be how we will get him out again,' Hope said, alarmed. 'We cannot let the poor thing die in the woodwork.'

'Perhaps a hole could be created,' Mr Drake said. 'Shall I tell Chilson to find a footman and a stout hammer?'

Hope looked at him in horror. 'I did not mean that we should pound holes in a building that does not belong to us.'

'We could bait him out, perhaps,' her husband countered.

'Or we can simply show some patience,' Charity said, exasperated with all of them. 'He is not stupid, you know. He will come out on his own, given time.'

'Because of you, we do not have time,' Faith snapped at her. 'The Earl is already angry with us. What will he say when he discovers that we have lost his dog?'

'He will probably shout for joy,' Charity said, annoyed. 'Now stop talking as if he is Grandfather and you must all walk on eggs to please him. You have married out of the family. If he is cross with you, you can simply turn and walk out that door, never to see him again.'

They could. But she was in the same state she had always been, utterly dependent on a man who did not respect her and with no rights to plan her own future. Worse yet, she had stripped herself naked for him, both figuratively and literally. She had no idea how to defend against someone who knew her as well as Potts did.

The barking seemed to be getting closer.

Then there was a hollow creaking sound and a shower of paint chips as a panel fell from the wall beside the main stairs and the Earl of Comstock emerged from the opening, hair and coat covered with plaster dust and face crimson with anger.

'Miss Strickland, I have found your damned chapel.'

For a moment, Charity could do nothing but stare at the man in front of them. He had been handsome enough before, but with his reasonable temperament she had never imagined he would amount to anything better than a lifetime as a clerk or secretary. He had looked like the sort of fellow that one saw adjacent to the men of real power. But as a sword might have been tempered by fire, a few hours trapped in the bowels of the house had turned him into a peer. He was in a towering rage worthy of anything her grandfather had managed when she had disobeyed him.

In the face of his ire, the entire family instinctively resorted to formality and respect, bowing and dropping curtsies, and greeting him as 'My lord', although the words coming out of Hope's mouth sounded more like a prayer.

They needn't have bothered. By the look in his eyes, Charity was the only one that he was angry with. But she was having none of it. She still stood firmly on the side of the little dog that had rushed out of the wall after him and would have bristled her hackles, had she been given any.

He pointed a cobweb-covered finger in a dire gesture worthy of a spectre, then shouted, 'You locked me in!'

'And you sold off my library,' she shouted back.

He gave a bitter laugh. 'After all your fine talk about liquidating the estate, you care about a few books? And it is not your library, it is mine.'

'So that is the way it's to be?' she said, raising her eyebrows and waving her arms. 'Everything is yours now, is it?'

'It is,' he said. 'Debts and all. And everyone thinks I am supposed to manage you, as well.'

'Do not think that means you can dictate my life to me,' she snapped. 'If you try, I will make you regret the day you left Philadelphia.'

'I already did regret it,' he countered. 'But I had no idea that, given the chance, you would try to kill me as Cyril killed poor Averill.'

'Kill you?' she laughed back at him.

'You might as well have had me thrown in an oubliette. No one could hear me screaming. Had I not found my way out of that room, I might have starved to death.'

'You missed tea,' she mocked. 'But please, tell me the agonies you suffered.'

'And then you set the dog on me. I was trapped in the walls with him.'

'The dog found you on his own. And you deserved whatever he did to you,' she said. 'You lied to me. From the first breath out of your mouth. You lied.'

'Not in everything,' he said. His voice changed, not quite softening, but displaying some new emotion beyond anger.

'You lied in all the things that matter,' she snapped back. 'How can I trust anything you say, Lord Comstock, or do you still expect me to call you Potts?'

'Miles,' he corrected.

'Ha! You did not even give me your Christian name when we...' she was suddenly conscious of the family about them, watching the argument in rapt fascination '...when we spent so much time together.'

'You were the one who decided I was an auditor,' he said.

'Because I did not believe that there was a man on the planet who was so awful that his own dog would hate him,' she said. 'I should have trusted Pepper's opinion of you and stayed far, far away.'

'He was away from me because I sent him,' the Earl said. 'Just as I should have done with you, instead of thinking that I could reside in the same house with you for a single day without being driven to madness.'

'I drove you mad?' She laughed. 'I made an honest mistake and you ran with it.' Then she turned to glare at the rest of the family. 'And when you all arrived, you all knew. Didn't you? You knew and you continued to allow me to be misled.'

'It was quite funny,' Faith said, unable to contain her smile. 'You have always been so smart. And yet you were so wrong in this.'

'So you took the opportunity to laugh in my face over it,' she said. 'I hope you all feel better for it. But you have proved that there is not a single person in this house I can trust.' She gestured to the dog. 'Come, Pepper, we are going to our room.'

But the dog, who had been her loyal companion only a week ago, ran to Comstock, wagging his tail.

'Very well, then, Judas, I will go alone,' she said, staring down at the dog in disgust. Then she turned and walked, back straight and eyes dry, up the main stairs to her bedroom.

Chapter Twenty

The discreet knock sounded on the Tudor Room door as Miles was attempting to brush the last of the brick dust from his coat.

'Come,' he shouted and immediately regretted it. After the very public argument in the hall below, he did not want to see any member of the Strickland family, ever again.

The door opened and Greg Drake stuck his head in, eyes lowered in deference as one might do when facing an angry lion. 'My lord, I have come to offer the services of my valet to help restore your clothing, after recent events.'

'I am fine on my own,' Miles said, with a vigorous scrub that seemed to be working the grime deeper into the wool.

'And your boots have become scuffed,' Drake added in a tone normally reserved for a death in the family.

'They are fine,' Miles snapped.

'Are you sure? Because Hagstead has a trick with

blacking and champagne that will have the most tired leather shining like a mirror.'

This was Drake's polite way of telling him that an earl was not supposed to take care of his own basic needs. He was supposed to be combed and curried like a show pony, too delicate to do as much as tie his own neckcloth. He had been getting such hints since the moment he'd stepped off the boat and he was damned tired of them.

But today he put down the brush, pinched the bridge of his nose and sighed in defeat. 'Very well. He can come before supper. There is no reason for him to waste his effort sooner since I will be going back into the walls.'

'Going back?' Drake was clearly baffled. 'Perhaps with the help of a servant…'

Miles tried to laugh, then stopped. It hurt. 'No, thank you. I would like to make it back out of the walls in one piece.'

'About that…' Drake gave a nervous cough. 'Chilson is here in the hall and wishes to speak to you.'

'The more the merrier,' Miles said with another sigh and a mockingly beneficent wave of his hand. 'Come in, Chilson. Speak your piece.'

'My lord.' The butler came into the room, knees wobbling and with a face as chalky white as Miles's had been before he'd wiped the dust from it. 'I take full responsibility for the incident that occurred this morning. Hoover would never have come above stairs, much less do what he did, had I not encouraged him. Nor would he and Biggs have locked you in a bedroom had they not assumed that it was what Miss Charity wanted done.'

'She did not ask them to?' It was probably an oversight. Now that she knew his real name, she was more than willing to lock him up and lose the door key.

'They misunderstood an instruction. Hoover is beside himself.'

'Better that than that he is beside me,' Miles said, grimacing.

'He truly is the gentlest of men.'

Miles rubbed his ribs. 'Do tell.'

'And good with the horses.'

'He should be. He is almost as large as one.'

'And kind to children, as well. He has six of his own,' Chilson added with urgency.

'What do his children have to do with this?' Miles asked Drake, annoyed. 'Are they going to hit me, too?'

'You are new to England and to the peerage. Perhaps you are not aware of the laws and etiquette that accompany your title.' Drake gave another quiet cough. 'As an example, should I have a reason to strike you—' he held up a hand of denial '—which I do not, of course. But if I struck you it would be a much more serious matter than brawling with some other gentleman. The punishment would be more severe, as well. And if a man of a lower class should assault you…a servant for example…' Drake stared at him, waiting for him to understand.

'He thinks I am going to have him hanged,' Miles said in disgust. And Chilson had come to plead for mercy and claim the punishment so that there would not be a family of orphans crying in the stables. 'This entire country is mad.'

'Perhaps,' agreed Drake. 'But we must make the best of it, mustn't we?'

Not for much longer, if he had any say in his future. But the current problem could not be solved by running away. Miles grabbed Chilson by the arm and pulled the quaking man into the room to a bench by the window. 'Sit.'

'Yes, my lord.'

Then he reached into his coat-tail and removed the flask he kept hidden there. He uncorked it and handed it to Chilson. 'Drink.'

'My lord?'

Miles tipped it up and poured some courage into the butler. 'Cherry bounce. A favourite of General Washington. Perhaps, you would have won the war had you some of this.'

It was probably not what he should say to a man who'd threatened his life. But at least the colour was returning to the butler's face. Chilson sputtered once, then helped himself to another sip. 'Thank you, Lord Comstock.'

Miles looked wistfully at the flask as the last of his American liquor disappeared into the butler. 'Now there will be no more talk of punishment for Hoover, who was only following orders.'

Chilson gave a relieved nod.

'I cannot fault any of you for decisions made in ignorance of my name and title, especially when I was the one keeping you in the dark.'

'Thank you, my lord,' said the butler, obviously curious but unable to ask him the reason for the deception.

'And you were acting in the best interests of the family and trying to protect Miss Charity.' Miles's throat tightened at the thought of her and the loathing with which she had greeted his true identity. 'I hope you will continue to do so, even when I am not present.'

'Of course, my lord,' the butler said and rose, back as stiff as ever and eyes clear despite the cloud of cherry brandy on his breath.

Miles did not bother to force him down to his chair again. Clearly, it had made the servant uncomfortable to be seated in the presence of a peer and some habits were not worth breaking. 'Very good, Chilson. Share my thanks with the rest of the staff for their hard work. And my apologies to you and to them for my deception.'

There was the faintest look of horror in Chilson's eyes at having to receive an apology, since Miles suspected that peers were never sorry for anything. But the butler accepted it with a 'Thank you, my lord.'

'And tell them to return my luggage from wherever they have taken it.'

The butler winced again. 'The duck pond, my lord.'

'Really?'

'It was thrown there after the silver was removed. The maids are drying your linen as we speak.'

'That is most kind of them,' he said. 'You may go.'

'Thank you, my lord.' At the dismissal, Chilson turned and disappeared in a cloud of subservience.

When Miles turned back, Drake was still in the

room. 'You may go, as well, Drake,' he said with a mocking wave of dismissal. 'I am fine here. Everything is fine.'

'The hell I will,' Drake said, his respect falling away now that he was sure no one was going to die. 'You are planning to go back to America, aren't you?' The man was looking at him as if his intentions were written plain on his forehead.

'What makes you think so?' Miles said, collapsing on the bench the butler had vacated.

'Charity claimed you were, but none of us could believe the fact. I assured them that you were making plans to get the estate in order. I said that it could not possibly be true.'

'So what if I am?' Miles replied. 'I have not learned much about this country, since I arrived. But I know that you have nothing to say in what a peer does or does not do.'

'True,' Drake agreed. 'But I also know that her sisters will not take kindly to finding that you have trifled with Charity's affections and then abandoned her. We will be forced to do something about it.'

After what Drake had just told him about the dangers of threatening an earl, it was an act of impressive bravery. It was also pointless. 'The notion that it is possible to trifle with Charity Strickland proves just how little you know her,' Miles said, shaking the abandoned flask into his mouth, trying to drain the last few drops from it. 'Next you will accuse me of breaking her heart, which is just as unlikely, since it is made of cold iron.'

But her body had been softer than he'd ever imagined. He shook the flask again.

'That is hardly a way to talk about a lady.'

'Perhaps not,' Miles said with a sigh. 'But in her case, it is accurate. Before she knew who I was, she made it quite clear that she wanted me to leave. What might or might not have happened between us meant nothing to her. And after?' He winced, thinking of the scene in the hall. 'I did not see any sign that her opinion has changed.'

'It does not matter what she wants,' Drake reminded him. 'You are the Earl of Comstock. Your place is here. Since you are the head of her family, her place is wherever you say it should be. Tell her to stop behaving like a child and accept your offer.' Drake paused, realising that he'd overstepped his bounds again. 'If you mean to offer, that is.'

It was exactly what she had feared would happen from the first and why she had hated him before she'd ever met him. And why she hated him even more, now that she realised that she had been lied to, manipulated and made to look like a naïve fool in front of the entire family.

'You are right. I am the head of the family and can do just as I please. And what I mean to do is return to America. Charity is quite capable of managing the estate in my absence and I shall leave her to it. If there are papers that must be drawn up to give her the authority, see that it is done. Then book me passage on the next ship to Philadelphia.'

He stood and brought his hands down the front of

his coat in a vicious swipe, to shake the last of the dust of England from it, along with the memory of the previous night. 'But before that can happen, she and I have a matter to settle that cannot wait another day.'

Chapter Twenty-One

It was not the first time that someone had knocked on her bedroom door that afternoon. But this knock was, by far, the most persistent. As she had done with all the others, Charity ignored it, along with all entreaties to 'open the door and listen to reason'.

Though she could not avoid the family for ever, it should not be unreasonable to lick her wounds in private for a little while longer. The mirth at her expense had been bad, but the pity that followed it was likely to be even worse.

And it was totally unneeded. There was no logical reason to mourn the loss of a man who had never existed. She had always known that there would be no future with Potts. The fact that he had been nothing more than a fictional construct made it better, not worse. She could preserve the time they had spent together like dried flowers under glass. As long as she took care to avoid the scoundrel who wore his face, she would be as content with the memory of him as she had expected to be when he had returned to his fiancée in Philadelphia.

'Go away,' she called to the person on the opposite side of the closed door.

The knocking stopped. Then she heard the key turn and the door open.

She glared at the Earl of Comstock as he crossed the threshold and closed the door behind him. 'I did not give you leave to enter.'

'I do not need it,' he said, jingling the ring of keys in his hand.

'I do not wish to see you, or speak with you, ever again.'

'I am endeavouring to make that possible,' he said. 'As you might remember, the Comstock coffers are near to empty. If we do not finish what we have begun, we will be forced to share this house for the sake of economy.'

'I thought you meant to sell my books,' she said, thinking of the empty crates in the library that were probably filled and on their way to London.

'Some of them,' he agreed. 'I have been living amongst Puritans and Quakers the whole of my life. I begin to see why they emigrated. They would have thrown the Comstock pornography collection into the fireplace to keep it out of the hands of impressionable girls.'

'Do not speak of me as if I am an absent child,' she snapped.

'I apologise,' he said, without sincerity. 'You are no longer a child. No one knows that better than I.' The admission was made without passion, but it hung in the air between them like a fog of musk.

Then he continued as if nothing had changed. 'I mean to sell the more prurient works collected on this shelf, along with the scrimshaw in the billiard room and a collection of lurid ivory figurines I discovered in one of the unused bedrooms. The items are barely legal and cannot be displayed in public and I have no interest in keeping them. But there are private collectors who will pay a pretty penny to own them.' He paused. 'Drake had been instructed to leave your shelf of favourite books in the library untouched and it will be quite some time before I need to cull the rest of the collection for valuable works. If you desire to keep any of the ones I wish to sell, all you need do is say so.'

The solution was so reasonable she'd have thought it had come from Potts. Thanks were probably in order, but she could not bring herself to give them.

'But that might be nothing more than a temporary solution,' he said. 'To be sure of the future, it would be better that we go to the chapel and collect the diamonds. If they are still there, that is.'

'I have no reason to search for them, now that you are here,' she said, all but tasting the bitterness as her ruined plans were used against her.

'You do not want your share?' he said.

'Do not taunt me with them,' she said. 'Now that Comstock knows of the plan, he will keep them for himself. There is nothing for me to collect.'

'And now you are speaking of me as if I am not in the room. Nothing has changed in me but my name. You were prepared to take a modest amount of the total. I see no reason to disagree with that.'

Oh, Potts.

It was his reasonable voice and logical solution that had spoken to her from somewhere inside this stranger. No matter what the rest of England thought, the Earl was a pale imitation of the man she had fallen in love with.

'Unless you are no longer interested in the search,' he said, becoming Comstock again. 'Then I will go get them myself and do as I will with them after.'

He was wrong. Something in him *had* changed, more than his name, for this was exactly how she expected an earl to behave. The moment she'd resisted him, he had issued an ultimatum.

When she did not answer, he added, 'You are not the least bit curious to see what I have found? Because what I discovered will fascinate you, even if you find my company intolerable.'

Damn him. He knew just how to pique her interest. She did want to see what he had found. Especially if his assessment of it was accurate.

'Think about it,' he said. 'And if you come to your senses, meet me in the bedroom where I was trapped. Then I will show you the secrets that lie between these walls.'

He had won again. It did not matter that he had lied and in doing so had ruined the happiest week of her life. He had hinted that the diamonds were as good as found and promised her the share that she had meant to take all along.

Still, she might have resisted, if he had not seemed

so very like Potts. But that did not mean she was going to continue to put on airs for him. She returned to her room and changed into her drabbest gown, then covered her hair in a mob cap that Dill claimed was only fit for an old lady.

The end result screamed her lack of interest louder than words could. But to be sure that there could be no doubts as to what she thought of him, she brought his dog.

When she arrived at the room, she found the door already open. By the sound of creaking floorboards she had heard as she approached, the Earl had been pacing. He froze when he saw her, then clasped his hands behind his back as if he could not quite decide what to do with them. 'I feared you would not come.'

He was making it seem like some romantic assignation and not an act of financial necessity. 'Well, I am here now. As is Pepper.' She stood back and waited for the attack that would put him in his place.

Instead, the dog ran forward and sniffed at him, wagging his tail once before losing interest and examining the hem of a nearby curtain.

'He did not try to bite you,' she said, amazed.

'We made our peace earlier today,' the Earl said. 'Later, when he found me wandering in the passages between the walls and he finally had his chance to do me real harm, he led me to an exit.' He stared pensively at the dog. 'He is not such a bad little fellow, I suppose. But if he has decided that I am to be master of this house, he is mistaken. My plans to leave have not changed.'

'The lovely Prudence,' she said, surprised to find that her bitterness on the subject had not abated now that she had learned his identity.

'If you think that her looks have anything to do with this, you are wrong,' he said. 'If you met her, you would say she is thick as two short planks. I proposed to her once, shortly after Ed died. But it was done out of duty to be sure she was looked after. There was nothing more to it than that. She did not like my prospects and refused. I was not good enough for her, you see.' He shook his head, in disgust. 'Her opinion of me changed quick enough when she learned of the title.' He gave her a sad smile. 'You might be surprised to know that not everyone is as set against marrying Comstock as you are.'

Of course they weren't. A single earl was a sought-after commodity on the marriage mart. To find one as young and handsome as the new Comstock would be like planting catnip outside a fish market. 'I do not doubt your attractiveness. To some people,' she added.

'When I refused to renew my suit, she became pregnant with another man's child.'

'Apparently, she is not quite so stupid as you thought.' The trap was so cleverly sprung that she almost felt sorry for him.

'She knows I will not break my promise. But she thinks that she can force me into bringing her to England as my wife. I do not care for monarchy, or inherited government. But I will be damned before I make her a countess and her bastard the next Earl. I decided that it would be better for the family if I went back to where I came from and did not let my problems affect the succession.'

If his description of her was accurate, the logic of his decision was sound. She would rather the family had no head at all than see all they had built placed into the hands of Prudence and her bastard child. 'You planned to disappear,' she said.

'And I would have, had I not run into you at the dower house.'

'And then I mistook you for someone else,' she said.

'I apologise for allowing the mistake to continue,' he said, with an embarrassed dip of his head. 'I did not intend to be here more than a day or two.'

In truth, it had been four. But it felt like she had known Potts for a lifetime. And now he was gone. 'It is over now. Let us speak no more about it.' Perhaps he'd expected some formal acceptance of his apology. But as yet she had no such thing to offer him. The hurt was still too fresh. 'Now, what did you wish to show me?'

'I found a way into the family chapel,' he said. 'And you are well dressed to go there for it is not an easy trip.' He walked across the room and handed her a lit lantern and a cloth sack containing candles, a tinder-box, paper and a pencil, and an assortment of small tools. 'This time, I mean to be better prepared,' he said and added, 'Here, you. Get off,' as Pepper began worrying at the second bag.

In response to the scold, the dog gave a happy yip and darted away from it to disappear under the bed.

The bedstead was already angled away from the wall and, with some effort, he pushed it further, revealing no sign of the dog. But there was a piece of panelling behind the headboard that appeared to be loose.

She hurried to it and pried at the edge, calling for the dog, and starting in after him.

'Not so fast,' he said, catching her arm before she could climb through the hole. 'Pepper has more lives than a cat and knows these passages far better than we do. But it could be rather dangerous. It would be wise to let me lead the way.'

Then he tugged at the panel and it swung away from the wall to widen the gap. He picked up the second bag and lantern with one hand, then stepped into the wall and offered his free hand to her. 'Stay close behind me and hold your lantern high.'

She jumped as the panel swung shut behind them, sealing them into the hallway between the walls. She held the lantern up as he had suggested, examining the space around them. On one side was the stone wall of the old house, on the other, the brick and timbers of the new.

'When I realised that you were not coming to release me, I decided to find my own way out,' he said, as if it were no mean feat to discover hidden passages that were unknown to the family. 'I wandered in the dark for what felt like hours. Then Pepper found me and led me to an exit. I suspect he has been chasing mice through the walls.'

Then he pulled a ball of string from the bag he carried. 'It will be easier by lantern light. But this should help if we lose our way.' Then he walked forward, letting the string spool out behind them as they proceeded.

She did not think his object in bringing her here had been to make her sorry for abandoning him. Even so, he succeeded. The space they were in was overhung with cobwebs and thick with dust. Though it did not overly bother her, a skittish girl would have screamed at the spiders, or run from the bats that sometimes fluttered out of the gloom. More than once, Comstock had been forced to stop short and work his way around missing floorboards that revealed dark, seemingly bottomless gaps.

But his first trip through this maze had been done in complete darkness. No wonder he had shouted at her in the hall. He might have been killed by accident and his body lost for ever.

They'd reached the end of a corridor and he turned to the right, then held up a warning hand. 'Be careful. The steps to the main floor are steep. We are lucky that they bothered with them, instead of leaving us with a ladder.'

When they reached the bottom of the stairs, she looked back. The walls of the next passage rose high on either side of them, twice as high as the last ones had been. 'We are near the old ballroom, I think,' he said.

'How did you know without a lantern?' she said.

'I found the steps by falling down them,' he said. 'And the ballroom by the echo.'

'And the chapel?' she said, baffled, as they turned a corner.

'Because, as you told me before, the Stricklands never throw anything away.'

'Oh.' Her jaw dropped in surprise.

Even a blind man might have known that was what he had found, but it was even more amazing in the dim light of their lanterns. 'I thought that they had blocked it off and torn it down. Or that perhaps it had been turned into a bedroom, or a parlour.'

'Because it makes no sense to subsume one building inside another,' he said, the lantern light wavering as he shook his head. The floor of the passage they stood in was littered with slates from a roof that angled away, a few feet above their heads, the slope ending where the foundations had been nailed for what was probably the musicians' gallery for the ballroom on the left. Stretching in front of them to the right was the outer wall of the chapel, complete with the deep stone sills of the stained-glass windows, the faces of saints in their leaded panes unreadable in the gloom.

'It is even more incredible, now that I can see it,' he said, his reverent voice echoing in the strange space. He tugged her hand and led her to another hallway around the corner that held a pair of iron-bound doors, set with large rings for handles.

'Have you gone inside?' she whispered.

'I was waiting for you,' he said, whispering back. Though they were alone, there was something about the space that demanded respect. He cleared his throat and spoke in a normal tone. 'But I doubt it is locked. What reason would there be for it?'

He reached into his bag again, removing an oil can and a pry bar. Then he went to work, greasing the hinges before taking one of the rings in his hand, twisting and pulling. The door creaked, moved a few inches, then stuck in the rubble on the floor around them.

As he put the pry bar to work, Charity crouched at his feet to clear away the debris. They worked well together, without the need for questions or orders. It was a shame that he had to go.

Then she remembered what she'd forgotten. He was not going anywhere. The man she wanted was already gone. Or perhaps not. As she stared up in the dim light, his features seemed to change from familiar to strange and back again.

Suddenly, the door gave way and he grabbed her hand, pulling her out of its way. He gave the hand he was holding an encouraging squeeze. 'Are you ready, Miss Strickland?'

He was being formal with her again. She'd thought, after last night, that had ended. And now that he was not Potts, what was she to call him?

He raised an eyebrow, waiting for an answer.

'Yes,' she said.

'Ladies first.' Now he held the lantern high, for her.

The space inside had a different kind of stillness, the noise of their breathing amplified by the confines of the room. The lights they carried could not seem to fill the space, leaving the ceiling and corners in darkness. Charity pulled the candles from her own bag, lighting first one, then another off the lantern. 'Let me see if I can find a place for these.'

She walked forward into the room, bumping against a bench before adjusting her course to put the doors at her back and pacing forward to find the altar. When she felt the corner of the table in front of her, she tipped the candle on its side to drip a pool of wax to fix it in, then stopped. Two more paces brought her to a branched candle stand with enough sockets for the rest of the tapers in her bag.

She lit them and fitted them in their places, then looked around her at the room revealed by the retreating darkness.

'Astounding,' Potts said, in a hushed tone. 'And you did not know this was here?'

'No one did,' she said, holding up her hands to indicate the room. Behind her, there was a marble altar, at least six feet long, on a raised dais with the metal stand that they had seen in the Blue Earl's portrait. On either side of her stood three rows of pews, stretching the length of the room towards the doors through which they'd entered.

Above them, the ceiling vaulted up and away into the darkness, the roof still largely complete. The angles gave the illusion that the space was much bigger than it probably was. But still, it was hard to contemplate how the room had been hidden.

They would need to illuminate the hallway, she thought. A series of candles to light them from the outside would make it possible to see the pictures in the windows.

She frowned.

The family had managed without a chapel for generations. There was no need of one now. Even if there was, there was no one left to marry at Comstock Manor. Even if his Prudence talked him into returning, Charity doubted that she would be willing to settle for anything less than St George's in Hanover Square.

'Do you remember the clue?' he asked.

'Right, left, right and left, three, four, two, one.'

'Alternating the two things, we have three to the right, four to the left and so forth.' He stamped his foot on the flagstones at their feet. 'But we must find a starting point.'

Charity retrieved her lantern and swung it low, searching the floor. 'Here.' She scuffed the dust from a brass cross, set in a stone at the base of the dais.

'Do we face towards the Bible, or away?' he wondered.

'Towards, I should think.' She shrugged. 'To be polite.'

'Very well, then.' He counted for her and she paced off the stones, only to stumble as she reached the last one.

Because it was loose.

She stared at him in surprise, then pointed down, too excited to talk.

He came to her side, staring down at it and then back to her again. 'Before I turn over this stone, we must talk.'

'I cannot imagine a thing you might say that is more important than the fate of our future,' she said, pointing down at their feet.

'You might be surprised to know that time will continue to pass even without the presence of the Comstock diamonds.' Perhaps it was a trick of the light, but he looked older than he had when they had left the bedroom. 'Have you thought of what you will do if we turn over the stone and find nothing?'

Just the thought of another failure made her throat tighten. It felt like the beginning of tears. But she refused to cry over disappointments. There had been many of them in her life and crying had not done a single thing to change them.

'What would I do? I would go back to the library and continue to search,' she said. 'They must be here. All the clues we have found point to the spot.'

'But suppose they have already been found,' he said. 'Perhaps they were sold long ago. What will you do if we discover that all there is to the estate is what you know there to be: debt and difficulty?'

'What would I do?' she said, staring at him in the gloom. 'You speak as if there is a decision to be made.'

'There always is,' he said softly.

'For men, perhaps,' she replied. 'My only decision will be whether I should depend on Faith and her husband, or Hope and hers.' In either case, she would become the spinster that her sisters had always expected. After what had happened between them, she could not imagine marrying another man. 'It is not as if I can remain here,' she added.

'You love this house,' he reminded her. 'When you spoke of it before, your only fear was that I would come and dictate your life to you should you remain. I told you then and I tell you now, that will not be the case. You are free to do as you like, whether I am here or not. And can stay here until you die,' he replied.

'To what purpose?' she snapped. 'There is no reason for a Comstock Manor, if you are not here to live in it.'

'You have always known that I would leave,' he said, surprised at her anger.

'I knew that Potts meant to leave.' The thought of that had been painful enough. 'But I had no idea that the Earl meant to abandon...everything.'

Me.

After all she had promised, before they'd made love, she had almost accused him of the very thing she swore she would not mind. But that was when she had assumed that there would be an earl eager to rule over her. She had hated the thought of it, willing to do anything to prevent it. But it had never occurred to her that a time might come when there would be no one at all to rebel against.

It was terrifying. Before she had known he was Comstock, she had been prepared to beg him to stay with her. But he had made his decision based on what was best for the earldom. It was the one area that she was sure she had no right to interfere with. If she did, she would tell him that yoking himself to this beautiful, American schemer was the height of stupidity. 'What will I do when you are gone?' she said at last. 'I can only tell you what I will not do. I will not sit alone, weeping over the loss of you. If you intend to go back to America, you had best get about it. Now lift the stone so we can see if your trip will be financed on diamonds or silverware.'

'Very well,' he said, scuffing the flagstone with the toe of his boot and watching it shift. 'There is nothing more to say.' Then, he walked back to the door and retrieved the pry bar, fit it into the widest open crack and lifted.

For a moment, they stared down into the hole he'd opened, stunned.

Then he said, 'Well, this is unexpected.'

Chapter Twenty-Two

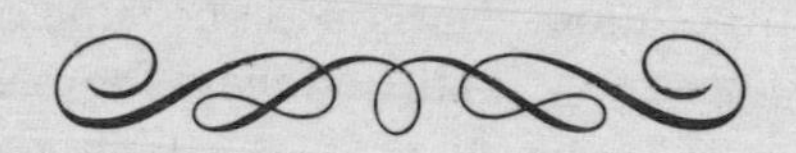

'Chilson!' Miles tried to keep the manic tone from his voice. Earls were not supposed to panic when they located the family fortune hidden under the floorboards. It probably happened all the time in England.

When he had moved the loose flagstone, he had assumed that, with luck, there would be a jewellery box, or perhaps a small sack containing the loose stones. They would have a moment of celebration as he counted out five of the best of them into her hand to show that the new Earl was not the demanding ogre she'd expected, just a perfectly reasonable fellow who honoured his bargains. If they could not be lovers, maybe they could at least be friends again.

But their search for the Comstock jewels had been more successful than they'd ever thought possible. Instead of a single pouch of diamonds, there had been several bags of jewellery, several small boxes of loose stones and a large metal strongbox full of coins. Cyril Strickland had not just hidden the family jewels from looters, he had amassed a dragon's hoard of gold and jewellery, then tucked it up under a stone and bricked off the room for good measure.

And then he had died and the world had moved on without him.

After a single, silent glance of agreement, they'd emptied the sacks they'd been carrying and begun to refill them with loot. But it soon became clear that they could not carry it all, and they'd agreed to take just enough to dazzle the rest of the family at dinner. Then he'd replaced the flagstone and led the stunned Charity out of the netherworld between the walls using the passage that led to the main hall.

Having recovered his composure after their earlier meeting, Chilson was there to greet them, freshly combed and starched, ready to serve.

Miles grinned at him. 'Yesterday you promised me footmen with hammers. Bring them here, please. And Hoover the groom, as well. I need muscle to demolish a wall.' It made no sense to be creeping through the house with a lantern, when there was a direct route available through the blocked archway in the ballroom.

Once he had explained to the butler what was required, Miles retired to his room to explore the damage done to his person and his wardrobe by the day's adventures. After its swim with the ducks, his clothing had been returned to the cupboard and seemed no worse for wear. But when he had stripped to wash, his body was a testament of scrapes and bruises from his run-in with Hoover and the time spent stumbling around in the walls. He would likely need help to get out of bed tomorrow once the stiffness had set in. Today, he was still numb.

He glanced at the stack of letters on the bureau that Drake had given him before everything had gone wrong. Damn Prudence, for introducing him to the idea that failure was even a possibility. He had been perfectly happy with how his life had been progressing until she had declared that he was not fit to marry her.

And now, when he had finally found a woman who was his equal, Pru had ruined it for him again. What had he expected Charity to say when he had questioned her in the chapel? Had he wanted her to proclaim her love for him and beg him to break his promise and stay with her?

It had not been her job to ask, it had been his to offer. He had been either too proud or too weak to say the words without some assurance that his proposal would be accepted. Perhaps it was just as well. Despite her many arguments to the contrary, she had spoken of the house being pointless without Comstock in it. If he had offered to stay and marry her, she might have accepted him against her better judgement, for the sake of the family.

But not for love. And without that, there was no point in remaining. If he wanted a loveless marriage, there was one waiting in Pennsylvania already.

He grabbed the letters, ready to throw them into the fire unread, then thought the better of it. If he truly meant to return home, he had best learn what fresh hell awaited him.

The first one he opened had been written while he

was still at sea. It was full of the same pleas for aid that the last letter had contained, interspersed with reminders of the difficulties she would face if Pru could not find a husband and the fact that her delicate condition grew more difficult to hide with each passing day.

The next letter was far more recent, dated several weeks after the proposal he had sent her on reading of her plight. In his letter, he had promised to help her and offered marriage, but explained there might be difficulties in getting home and the problems with the Comstock finances. He'd urged her to be patient and promised that he was returning as soon as he could gather enough money to clear Edward's debts, but would arrive well before the child would need his name.

Her answer to his three pages of promises took barely half a sheet of paper.

Only you could find a way to ruin an earldom.

There was more. But the gist of it stated that his return would not be necessary. His fancy title was worth nothing compared to cash on the barrelhead. She had dared to hope that the second Strickland might finally equal the first, but he had proved sorely disappointing.

To add insult to injury, the letter had been signed Mrs Prudence Parker, the surname of the banker who held Edward's notes. That man was middling handsome but, since he owned one of the largest houses in Philadelphia, a lack of hair and an excess of belly had made no difference, once Miles had been out of sight of land.

There was a third, somewhat longer letter from the banker Horace Parker, accusing him of abandoning a woman in need, and the child he had fathered. Apparently, Pru had been as thorough in her entrapment of Horace as she had been of him. Parker had dried her tears and settled her debts, and now made it clear that there was no room in Pennsylvania for a turncoat who would renounce his country and serve King George. They were all better off without him. Dire action would be taken should Horace hear that Miles had darkened American shores.

He sat on the bed for a moment, staring at the papers and trying not to grin. She had refused him again. He was free of his promise. Even the ghost of Ed Strickland could not expect him to come back and sort this mess out.

Somewhere deep inside him, there was a desire to return in triumph and prove her wrong. He ignored it. Only a fool would send an answering letter to Pru, announcing that she'd just made the biggest mistake of her life.

But if he was not wanted at home, and he was not wanted here, where did he belong? His plan to turn the estate over Charity was a sound one, but it was so much more complicated now that there was money to give her. Tonight, his mind was as numb as his body. Life was much more complicated than chess. He could not manage to see more than a single move ahead.

As he had not eaten since the night before, his opening gambit would have to begin with food of some sort. He rang for Drake's valet. In no time at all, Hagstead had worked miracles on him, his clothing and, as promised, his boots. Then, with a sigh of resignation, he went to the linen drawer and retrieved his signet again, slipping it on his finger before going down to dinner.

Tonight's menu was mutton, likely the best that the cook could manage when surprised by the arrival of four extra guests. But the ragout was as tender as lamb and Miles had sent word that the meal was to be accompanied by the finest wines in the cellar. Instead of the comfortable place halfway down the table with Charity, he sat at the head.

The family rose in respect as he entered. Even Charity, though she did so with downcast eyes. The sight made him wince. 'Please, sit,' he said, gesturing them back to their chairs. 'And the first one of you to call me "my lord" will be banished from the table.'

'And what are we to call you now? When you can't seem to keep a name from one day to the next, it is difficult to know what to do.' It was Charity, of course, the only one with nerve enough to speak her mind.

He smiled. 'Miles. It is my given name and, since you are my family, I would prefer that you use it.'

'Of course, my lord,' Charity replied.

Apparently, the familiar affection that they'd fallen into as they explored had disappeared at the sight of him sitting in her grandfather's chair. He would have no help from the rest of the family, who sensed the tension between them and began emptying their plates at a speed that made it impossible for them to speak.

'Thank you, Charity,' he said. No longer bound by formality, he could call her by the name he had only whispered as they'd shared a bed. 'Have you told your sisters what it was we discovered this afternoon during our exploration of the house?'

'I was waiting for you, Lord Comstock,' she said, her hands in her lap, her tone subservient and her eyes glaring a challenge.

He raised a hand to signal the footman standing at the door of the dining room and instructed him to go to the study and bring the bag that was sitting on the desk.

When it arrived, Miles rose to take it, then dumped the contents out on to the cloth. Forks dropped as gold coins spilled across the table, clinking against wine glasses. An emerald necklace slithered out after them to lay beside his plate like a snake.

He sat again and took a sip from his wine glass as though nothing unusual had happened.

'My Lord.' It was Leggett who spoke, clearly invoking the deity rather than his host.

'This is just a small portion of what we found,' Miles announced, revelling in the drama of the announcement. 'It was not possible to carry it all away. The servants have begun opening a passage to the chapel where it was hidden.'

Then he turned to Drake. 'This is likely to lead to some complications in the plan I put forth this morning to turn the management of the estate over to your sister-in-law.'

'What?' Charity's voice was sharp as a whip crack in the silence of the room.

Miles gave her a bland look. 'Though you insist that no Earl of Comstock would ever listen to your suggestions, your ideas so far have been as sound as anything I could come up with. When I left, I was planning to leave the running of the estate to you.'

For the first time since he had known her, she seemed too stunned to speak. It was strangely satisfying.

'Of course, there are problems with that now,' he said directly to Drake. 'Though it shall be easier for her to run things if there is enough money to do it, when we total up the booty, I suspect she has just become one of the most eligible heiresses in England. There will be a problem with fortune hunters, of course.'

'I am not an heiress,' she snapped. 'I am a distant relation to the Earl of Comstock. Perhaps you do not understand the principle of primogeniture.'

'I understand it. I simply do not agree with it,' he said, smiling down the table. 'America has been managing well without it for a generation or longer. I do not intend to come here and regress in my thinking. Like it or not, Charity, you and your sisters will receive a substantial share of the family fortune.'

'I don't understand,' she said softly. 'Why would you do such a thing?'

'Since the day I arrived, you have made it quite clear what you wanted from life. You wished for money of your own with which you could set up housekeeping. You wished for a sufficient dowry to attract a husband and to choose him for yourself. Most of all, you wished to be taken seriously by the Earl of Comstock.' He stared at her, willing her to understand what he had no intention of saying in front of the entire family, especially if he was not sure of her response.

'I am giving you everything you asked for. Just as I promised, when I was Potts, I am giving you the freedom to choose your own future. And I hope, the next time you choose a man, you will do a better job of it than you have this week.' Then he threw his napkin aside and left the table.

Chapter Twenty-Three

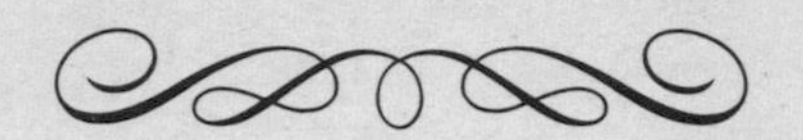

Once he was gone, the table erupted in conversation and demands that she describe the afternoon in detail, with particular attention to the size of the fortune they'd found. Was it truly as large as he'd said?

'Yes,' Charity said, staring down at her hands, which were folded tightly in her lap.

'How amazing,' Faith said, unable to contain her smile. 'And he means to share it with us. The man is kindness himself.'

'But Gregory told me he is going back to America,' Hope said urgently. 'It is not that we have not always suspected you were capable of running the estate. But you cannot take his seat in Parliament for him. Is there nothing you can do to persuade him to stay?'

'No,' Charity said firmly.

Ask him.

She ignored the perfectly reasonable suggestion in her own head.

'Nothing at all?' Faith said with a pointed expression, as if to hint that, though they did not know what the matter could be, they were sure it was her fault and that an apology might solve everything.

'He is going back to America because his fiancée is there,' Charity announced. It did not matter that he was marrying an unworthy trollop who was likely to make him miserable. He had made the offer and he was a man of his word.

'He is engaged?' Drake said, frowning. 'This is the first I have heard of it and I made some effort to discover his past.'

'Her name is Prudence. She is very beautiful,' Charity said, swallowing a bite of her pudding around the lump in her throat.

'And when did he tell you of her?' Faith said, eyes narrowing.

'From the first,' Charity answered. 'He made no secret of her.' He had lied about his name, but in all other things he had been completely honest with her.

'He was engaged. And yet he…' Hope's voice fell away as if she did not want to accuse him of something that could not be taken back.

'He did nothing,' Charity snapped. 'It was me. It was always me. He did everything in his power to avoid a liaison. But I badgered him until he succumbed.'

There was another profound silence at the table as the family tried to digest that they were not only speaking of something totally inappropriate for mixed company, but that it seemed to involve the youngest and supposedly most naïve member of the family instigating an affair.

At last, Mr Drake spoke. 'Though you may feel you

are to blame, your version of events is not accurate. He concealed his identity from you. If he had been honest, you might have felt differently towards him.'

Of course she would have. She'd have treated him as she had tonight, arguing, snapping and being difficult for no reason. She was as bad as Pepper, who had yapped and nipped, angry at the unfairness of the world and taking it out on the man who had rescued him. And Potts… Comstock…

Miles.

His true name seemed to resonate in her mind like the ringing of a bell. Miles had done nothing to deserve the dog's hatred. But that had not changed the way he behaved towards it. He had never kicked, never shouted, and gone out of his way to keep the dog safe and well, expecting nothing in return. It was the sort of nobility that one imagined for the peerage, but seldom found in real life.

Mr Leggett was unimpressed. 'No matter the provocation, he knew what he was doing was wrong. The onus lies with him to do right by you.' He had been a rake before falling in love with Faith. Apparently, it had taken only two months of marriage to her sister to turn him into a tiresome busybody, eager to spoil the fun for everyone else.

'We will speak to him,' Mr Drake added. 'And remind him that his duty lies with family first.'

'Prudence is his family, as well. She was his late brother's wife.' And she did not need Charity's help in getting or keeping the man she wanted. She had lied and cheated and won.

'A widow,' Mr Leggett said, as if this explained all. Mr Drake nodded.

'None of this matters,' Charity snapped, glaring around the table at him. 'Whatever has happened was between Comstock and myself, and is no business of any of you. You will not speak to him about his supposed obligation to me, nor will you question me about it. Not now. Not ever.'

And then, before she dissolved into the pointless tears that her family was expecting, she fled the room.

One of the advantages of living at Comstock Manor was that when one wanted to run away, one had plenty of space to do it in. She had been no more than four when they had first arrived and Charity had vague memories of wandering the endlessly long corridors, searching for her mother and weeping.

It had been years since she'd got lost. But tonight, she was tempted to try. At the very least, she could find a place to have a good cry in private, to give vent to her frustrations without having her brothers-in-law demanding satisfaction and her sisters forcing her down the aisle when she simply wanted to be left alone.

Since Comstock might have retired to the Tudor Room or the Earl's suite, she did not want to be anywhere near the bedrooms. It would be hard enough sleeping down the hall from him with a wing full of chaperons. She could not trust herself to be alone.

Instead, she ran down the centre wing to the back of the house and was halfway to the ballroom before she had realised what she was doing. Then she slowed. The sound of rhythmic pounding came from somewhere ahead, along with the incessant barking of Pepper, the dog. Perhaps the foolish creature had run back into the walls and was stuck. Though she did not relish the idea of navigating the tunnels in the dark, she could not stand the thought of leaving him for the night.

She walked on in the direction she'd been going, as the volume of the sounds increased. Then, as the back staircase widened to reveal the ballroom, she understood. At the end of the great room, the Earl of Comstock was stripped to his shirt sleeves, swinging an enormous hammer at what was left of the wall that blocked off the chapel. Pepper danced around his feet, barking in approval as he dodged out of the way of falling bricks.

Her beautiful Mr Potts, the American man of action. She could not help smiling as she walked down the room to stand at his side. 'If you think it so important that the job be finished tonight, you can call for servants,' she said, over the pounding of the hammer.

'I do not want help,' he said, scowling. 'Not from you, or anyone else.'

'You will not get more than advice from me,' she said, pulling a delicate gold chair from the stack along one wall and sitting to watch him work. Though she had told herself that she did not want to see him again, the view was hard to resist. His sweat-soaked shirt clung to his back, outlining muscle and sinew as he moved.

'I would prefer that you not give me that, either,' he

said, leaning on the hammer. 'You said that taking liberties with your person would have no permanent effect on either of us. What a load of hogwash that turned out to be. I'm in such a state that I'm breaking rocks after dinner so I can sleep at night.' He pointed an accusing finger at her. 'After the billiard room, you likely slept like an angel. But I ran through the upper halls like a madman until I was too tired to think about you. The night after that, you caught me hanging my hair splitter out the window to cool the thing off. And tonight?' He cocked his thumb at the loose bricks on the wall. 'I am knocking down walls.'

'Because of me,' she repeated.

He looked thoughtful. 'After I return to America, I suspect I will turn to lumberjacking. I have never tried it, but it looks like damned hard work.'

'Do they have forests in Pennsylvania?' she asked.

'They have forests in Maine,' he said. 'I am no longer welcome in Philadelphia.'

'What about Prudence?' she said, almost afraid to ask.

'Once she learned there was not likely to be much money in Earl-ing, she turned around and married a banker.'

'Then you are free,' she said softly.

'If you call this freedom,' he said, gesturing at the house around him.

'Now that there is money to run the place, I do,' she said.

'Then take it with my blessing,' he replied, as if it should make any sense at all.

'You still mean to go to home, though you do not have to?'

'You are here,' he said. The words should have hurt her. But there was a longing in the way he said them that made her heart flutter.

'If my presence bothers you, there is all the rest of England to hide in,' she said.

He shook his head. 'Not big enough. You could drop a dozen Englands into America and still not fill it up.'

The idea amazed her. 'I should rather like to see that.'

'If I am going away so I do not have to see you, your following me there defeats the purpose,' he said.

'You are trying to avoid me?'

'Does it matter? When we were in the chapel, you seemed more concerned about the absence of an earl than you were about losing me. Before that, you wanted me, but not the Earl. You cannot have one without the other, Miss Strickland.'

He had gone back to being proper. But rather than feeling cold and distant, the sound of her surname raised the colour in her cheeks. 'Now that I have met the Earl of Comstock, I think I could grow quite fond of him,' she said, smiling. 'And I will always have a soft spot for my dear Mr Potts, even if that is not his real name.'

'That is good to know. Because the more time I spent with you, the harder it was to imagine how I could ever be happy with someone else.' He let the hammer fall and walked towards her. 'It is rare that I have to exert myself when beating someone at chess. I suspect, once you have studied my play, it will become even harder.' Then he smiled. 'And I have never had an opponent with such distracting cleavage.'

'Was it the chess that decided you?' she asked eagerly. 'Because that was when I knew that I loved you.'

'Probably not,' he admitted. 'When I found you up a chimney, I was intrigued. Even more so after the chess game. But when I realised that you came with an entire library...' He shrugged, helpless. 'How could I not love a woman with so many books?'

'They are actually your books,' she reminded him.

'The family's,' he corrected. 'I still intend to share them with you. If you want them, that is,' he added. 'You are a rich woman now, Charity Strickland. Once word gets out that we are flush, you will have your pick of gentlemen. I will have to fight my way through the throng just to get to your billiard table.'

'You forget that you are an earl,' she said, smiling. 'I will not even bother talking to barons and misters. It would be just a few dukes and marquesses ahead of you in the line.'

'I did not think you were interested in titles,' he said. 'I'd have told you my name much sooner if I had not been sure that being Lord Comstock would count against me.'

'I suppose some earls are all right,' she allowed. 'But in my experience, English lords can be quite full of themselves.'

'Then it is a good thing I am not really English,' he said, pulling her into his arms for a kiss.

Epilogue

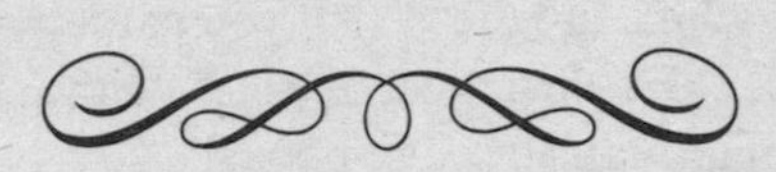

'Chilson! Where is my wife?' As his Countess had frequently pointed out to him, it was not really necessary to shout when calling the servants. There were bell pulls in every room. Even without a summons, they tended to hover close by, ready to help. Unless he took pains to shut them out of the room, there was usually a maid or footman close enough to hear him if he spoke in a normal voice.

But if he stood in the middle of the entry hall and shouted, there was an echo. It gave him an irrational pleasure to be able to hear how large his new home was, without even having to look at it. It was also an excellent position to admire the greenery that had been brought in to decorate the house for the Christmas season. He had insisted that the holly and ivy, mistletoe and hellebore were supplemented by a proper Christmas tree in the main parlour, decorated with fruits and nuts and gingerbread, and lit with candles just as he'd had back home.

'Lady Comstock is in the library, my lord.' Chilson arrived as he always did, seemingly out of nowhere and as staid and silent as Miles was loud. After almost ten months, the butler had grown used to his habits. Miles suspected that they amused him, if English butlers were allowed a sense of humour. It also seemed to please him that the woman who had arrived here as the smallest of three orphans was now a countess. He repeated her title whenever he could, as if unable to contain his pride. 'Lady Comstock is with the painter.'

Miles grinned. 'Then she will not mind being interrupted.' He bounded down the hall to find her. Even with the sudden influx of money to the estate, the library was as tatty as ever. The Christmas greenery on the mantelpiece could not seem to hold its leaves and the berries fell from the kissing bough in the doorway almost faster than they could pluck them off.

But it was Charity's favourite room and his, as well. He could not think of a better place for her to sit for her portrait.

He leaned forward and kissed his wife on the cheek and was rewarded with a hiss of disapproval from the artist.

'I will not move.' Charity sighed, then returned a rigid smile and muttered, 'He wants me to remove my spectacles.'

'I forbid it,' Miles said, using his earl's voice and enjoying the painter's flinch of subservience.

'And I would like to remove the tiara,' she said, making a face.

'I forbid that, as well,' he said in a much more affectionate tone. 'You may have talked me into waiting for the formal portrait. But if this miniature is to be my Christmas present, I reserve the right to choose your costume.'

'I lack the energy to stand for a full-length painting,' she reminded him. 'Perhaps when I am out of my confinement.'

He grinned at the mention of her delicate condition. 'I will insist on it.'

'And do not puff yourself up about the chances of getting an heir on the first go,' she said, still murmuring through an unwavering smile. 'Though you know much about advising the local farms in the care of their crops and animals, you have done nothing to grow this child.'

'I was there at the start,' he said, feeling quite smug about it. 'And I have been keeping its mother well fed and properly coddled. I have just come from speaking with the workmen. The family chapel will be in fine shape for the christening in spring. The windows are quite lovely, when lit from behind.'

'So there will be no risk of you stepping in holes in the floor, as you did at our wedding?' she asked.

'It is good that we spent the next week in bed,' he replied. 'My ankle was not quite right for some time after.'

'But it was strong enough as you danced last week,' she reminded him.

'When the whole family is gathered for a ball, one cannot sit out the dances,' he said. 'But we must see about cutting another doorway to the ballroom. The guest wings are looking much better, but it is a bother to have to walk through them to get there.'

'Next year,' she said, smiling.

As he dismissed the portrait artist for the day, she pulled off the jewellery she had been wearing, stretching her neck and rolling her shoulders as if the weight of them bothered her. For the first time in several generations, the Countess of Comstock would be wearing real diamonds in her portrait and Miles had requested that she deck herself in as much of the set as she could stand. They did nothing to make her more beautiful or precious to him, but he liked to be reminded of the fun they'd had in searching for them.

He stepped behind her to massage her shoulders, making her sigh in satisfaction. 'So you have enough energy to visit the village? A wagon has been loaded with baskets for the tenants and I am eager to be done before dark.'

She smiled. 'I am never too tired to play Lady Bountiful. It must amuse Faith and Hope to no end that I am finally developing manners and living up to my name.'

'Wise and generous,' he said with a proud smile, then kissed her ear and whispered, 'Beautiful, as well.'

By the way her skin coloured at the words, she still did not fully believe him. But she believed in his love. Believing in herself would come, with time.

'And has your surprise arrived?' she asked, turning to kiss him.

'Several barrels of it,' he assured her. 'Cook has poured it off into bottles. Every family on the property will have maple syrup for their Christmas dinner. And this is for you.' He pulled the napkin from his pocket and offered her the treat he was carrying there.

'Candy?' she said, taking a brittle string of sugar into her mouth.

'You cook the syrup down, then pour it out on to the snow to harden,' he said. 'Since nature will not cooperate and give me proper winter weather, I had to make do with a bowl of shaved ice. But there is plenty left to have over corn pudding with our dinner.'

She laughed and made a face. 'Maize mush for a holiday meal. Lord Comstock, you are an odd man. But I love you dearly and will clean my plate if it keeps you from returning home.'

'It is not my home, darling,' he said, kissing her again. 'America is just the place where I was born. My home is with you.'

* * * * *

If you enjoyed this story check out
Faith's and Charity's stories in the
Those Scandalous Stricklands miniseries:

'Her Christmas Temptation'
in Regency Christmas Wishes
A Kiss Away from Scandal

And why not check out these other great reads
by Christine Merrill?

The Secrets of Wiscombe Chase
The Wedding Game
A Convenient Bride for the Soldier

COMING NEXT MONTH FROM HARLEQUIN® HISTORICAL

Available December 18, 2018

All available in print and ebook via Reader Service and online

THE UNCOMPROMISING LORD FLINT (Regency)
The King's Elite • by Virginia Heath
Charged with high treason, Lady Jessamine is under the watchful eye of Lord Peter Flint. But Flint soon realizes tenacious Jess hides a lifetime of pain. Can he afford to take a chance on their attraction?

A MARRIAGE DEAL WITH THE VISCOUNT (Victorian)
Allied at the Altar • by Bronwyn Scott
After an abusive marriage, Sofia finally finds true safety in the arms of Viscount Taunton. But to leave her past behind, Sofia must consider his offer of full protection—in the form of wedding vows!

THE EARL'S IRRESISTIBLE CHALLENGE (Regency)
The Sinful Sinclairs • by Lara Temple
When Lucas, Lord Sinclair, receives a summons from Olivia, he's skeptical he can help restore her late godfather's reputation. But a new challenge quickly presents itself: keeping her at arm's length!

SENT AS THE VIKING'S BRIDE (Viking)
by Michelle Styles
To escape her brother-in-law and protect her sister, Ragnhild agrees to marry unknown warrior Gunnar Olafson. Only his belief in love died with his family. Can she melt her Viking's frozen heart?

A RAKE TO THE RESCUE (Regency)
by Elizabeth Beacon
Widow Hetta Champion and her little boy are endangered by her father's hunt for a murderer, and aristocrat Magnus Haile is compelled to assist! Could Hetta offer Magnus the family he's long believed impossible?

A VOW FOR AN HEIRESS (Regency)
by Helen Dickson
With a bankrupt and crumbling estate, Lord Ashurst needs a rich wife! He leaps at a marriage with heiress Rosa Ingram. But after discovering the truth about her family wealth, should he marry her?
